One Green Leaf

Almost from their first day at Clareville Comprehensive, the four of them had been friends: Abbey, Robyn, David and Zoot. Only in the sixth year did the pattern of their close friendship change—with Abbey and David becoming really serious about each other, while Robyn and Zoot were happy to be 'just good mates'.

In the summer term of that year, the unthinkable happens. It's always been Zoot who was accident-prone, but now it's David—golden boy David —who's suddenly missing from school, in hospital facing an urgent operation.

'What is so awful,' says Abbey, 'is the way everything else just seems so trivial.'

Out there in the world terrible, terrible things were happening . . . but Abbey's own, personal world had shrunk to a pinpoint. Yesterday she had been worried about the bomb and nuclear waste and radiation: today all she could think about was David.

Robyn tells the story of all the terrible—and wonderful—things that happened to the four friends during that memorable summer.

ALSO BY JEAN URE

One Green Leaf

JEAN URE

'An oak with but one green leaf'
—*Much Ado About Nothing*

THE BODLEY HEAD
LONDON

British Library Cataloguing
in Publication Data
Ure, Jean
One green leaf.
I. Title
823'.914 [F] PR6071.R7/
ISBN 0-370-30784-4

© Jean Ure 1987
Typeset by Wyvern Typesetting Ltd
Printed in Great Britain for
The Bodley Head Ltd
32 Bedford Square, London WC1B 3EL
by Cox & Wyman
First published 1987

1

I remember . . . so many things. So many, many things.

I remember our first day at school; the big school. Clareville Comprehensive. I remember seeing Abbey, standing by herself in a corner of the playground: very slender and upright, with an air about her even then of seriousness and calm. I remember envying her her two thick plaits of creamy-coloured hair (mine is coarse and curly and what is politely known as auburn, otherwise ginger), and the fact that even in school uniform she could manage to look neat without looking boring. I remember wondering if she was also new, and if so whether we might become friends —which of course we did.

I remember Zoot, dashing about with a football, with a gang of other boys. I didn't know it then, but they had all come up from juniors together and weren't isolated like Abbey and me. Abbey had only just moved to the district (her father, who was quite old, had kept a greengrocer's shop in Crawley and had now retired and come to the seaside for his health) whereas I had been at some dotty little private school from which everyone but me had moved on to bigger and more prestigious establishments where they might meet future princesses, or even train to become princesses themselves if that was what they fancied, only I didn't, I wanted to catch the 8.30 bus every day and go to Clareville Comprehensive, like a girl in our road, because ever since I could remember I'd thought that catching the bus and going into town all by oneself was just about the most romantic thing imaginable.

Unlike Abbey, who told me afterwards that she was terrified, I didn't mind not knowing anyone that first day; but then I'm different from Abbey. Beneath her cool exterior Abbey is actually quite shy, or perhaps reserved rather than shy, but anyway it takes her ages to get talking to people. I'll talk to anyone, and so will Zoot. He talked to me that first morning when he barged into me with his football—or at least, he paused long enough to grin and push his hair out of his eyes and say sorry, which is more than some of them would have done. I remember thinking two things: one, that as boys went Zoot didn't seem too bad—I'd hardly ever met any boys at that stage and was secretly rather looking forward to it, though naturally I wouldn't have said so—and two, that from the way he was carrying on, chasing up and down as if he owned the place, he must have been at the school some time.

It wasn't until a bell rang and we were told to fall into line, and Zoot fell in behind me (and was hardly any taller than I was, and I wasn't tall: he's overtaken me since, but not by that much) that I realized we were all in the same year. Same year, same class: me and Abbey, Zoot and David.

David arrived late. I remember him arriving. We'd all just got settled after the business of finding desks and sorting out who we were going to sit next to, and I'd managed to wangle it so I was sitting next to Abbey, which wasn't too difficult since most of the others had somebody they'd been to juniors with and naturally enough they tended to stick together, at any rate at the beginning.

Zoot and his mob had dug themselves in at the back

6

and were honking and hallooing and generally making mayhem. I remember the Great Rhetorical Windbag (except that in those days he was still known as Mr Harris: it wasn't till several terms later he became the Great Rhetorical) had just forcibly split them up, moving Zoot, as the likely prime trouble-maker, to the front of the class in a desk by himself; and I remember the door opening and David coming in.

I think it was then, at that moment, that the Great Rhetorical conceived his bitter loathing. I honestly think he took one look at David and just decided, right there and then, to have a thing against him. Of course, David didn't help matters *later* (neither did Zoot) but he hadn't done anything *then*. It was just the Windbag, having it in for him.

I remember the Windbag saying, 'And who might this be? Anyone one is supposed to know?' in a sneering sort of voice which actually is fairly natural to him, I mean he just is a naturally sneering sort of person. What he likes best is for people to wilt. Abbey would have wilted. Zoot and I would have got cheeky, and that would have pleased him almost as well because then he could have delivered one of his great rhetorical lectures about manners making man, and common courtesy, and all the rest. David went and spiked his guns by taking it absolutely seriously.

I remember him standing there, at the door, small and slight, which he was in those days (he grew taller later on, and filled out) saying very solemnly, 'I'm David James Geary and I live at Mailoo Farm and I don't *think* that you know me.'

I remember Zoot sniggering and the Great Rhetorical being not best pleased (which was something one could tell, even at the age of eleven) and trying to retrieve lost ground by resorting to sarcasm; demanding to know what, pray, was Master Geary's excuse for coming amongst us so late in the day? Mental black-out? Choking fit? Or simple inability to get himself out of bed? And I remember David, all innocent and clean-scrubbed – sort of angelic-looking, almost, with his quiff of dark hair and those incredibly blue eyes – earnestly explaining that it wasn't any of those things, 'It was the old sow, sir, giving birth.'

I remember the class just exploded. I remember some sexist nerd, one of Zoot's ex-cronies, yelling, 'You didn't oughta talk about your ma like that!' and Abbey turning bright pink (whether through embar-rassment or because she felt strongly even then about things like sexism and racism and all the other isms, I'm not really sure, though knowing Abbey it was most likely a mixture of both). The Great Rhetorical, who never *could* stand competition, even from eleven-year-olds, just snappishly told David that now he was here he'd better go and sit down; and directed him to the only vacant desk, which was the one next to Zoot's, which was how David and Zoot came to be friends.

There's nothing like sharing a desk on your very first day at a new school for promoting what Zoot likes to call mateship. I've noticed several cases even in just our own year where people who sat next to each other on that first day stayed together right up the school. Big Jane Dorning, for example, and Little Jane Waters; Pilch Maguire and Andrew Dove (whom David and Zoot always insisted on referring to as Andy Pandy for what they said were obvious reasons); and of course Abbey and me.

Funny about Abbey and me. Looking back on it, we didn't really have all that much in common. Abbey was always going to be something in science, I was always going to be an actress. The things that she was good at—maths, physics, chemistry—were the things that I was hopeless at; and the things which got *me* going—English and drama and end-of-term shows —on the whole left Abbey quite cold. But then it was the same with Zoot and David. Apart from the usual all-boys-together act, arms-around-the-shoulders and close-ranks-in-times-of-trouble, they didn't actually have any more in common than Abbey and me. David, like Abbey, was into science (he was going to be a vet, which was something he had decided when he was five years old) while Zoot was into nothing-in-particular and everything-in-general. Alone amongst us, Zoot never had the least idea of what he wanted to be. As far as I know, he still hasn't: he seems perfectly content just to be Zoot.

But in spite of our differences—differences in background, differences in outlook—we were just about as close, the four of us, as you could possibly hope to get. For a few weeks, at the beginning, there was Robyn (which was me) and there was Abbey, and there was David and there was Zoot. By the end of the first term we had become just two separate entities, RobynanAbbey, DavidnZoot. Later on, by about the end of the third year, a new entity was starting to emerge. This one was known as DavidnAbbey, and by the time we reached the fifth year it had almost completely taken over from the other two, though in the face of male chauvinism RobynanAbbey would still put in a united appearance, and there were always those odd masculine moments of hearty ho-ho-ness when DavidnZoot would burst forth upon us. There was never any RobynanZoot; not in quite the same way. We never became a one-together as the other two did. I don't think we ever really wanted it, we were happy as we were, me and Zoot, just being mates.

In the early days, of course, we all kept very firmly to our own sides of the great sexual divide. At the age of eleven, Abbey and I certainly didn't want to get mixed up with any boys. I remember thinking that Zoot was funny and that David was nice (whatever nice was supposed to mean—the fact that he wasn't rude or rough or dirty, perhaps) but it would never have occurred to us to go out with them or ask them back to tea.

I remember going to 'tea', very politely, with Abbey after we'd known each other a few weeks. I remember meeting her parents and thinking at first that they must be her grandparents, because Mrs Johnson had been nearly forty when she had had Abbey, and that made her very nearly the same age as my grandmother, which seemed to me rather shocking until I got used to the idea. Abbey, of course, never having known anything different, looked upon it as quite normal, though I think when she came back to tea at my place and met my parents, who were still pretty young as parents go, not a bit granny-or-grandpa-ish, she was a bit taken aback. She said she thought my mother was 'awfully glamorous' (the way she said it she almost made it sound as if a mother *oughtn't* to be glamorous) and for ages she was so paralysed with embarrassment in front of my father that out of kindness to her he used to leave the room whenever she appeared; though afterwards, when Abbey was going through her doctor phase and deciding that she was going to be a Brilliant Woman Physician (she later dropped that idea in favour of being a Brilliant Woman Physicist) they got on quite well and she even went along to the surgery once or twice in school holidays to help out.

Abbey's parents live in a semi on one of the new developments just outside the town centre: within easy reach of sea front and amenities, as they say in the brochures. Zoot's parents are right over the other side of town, down near the harbour—'poor but pictureskew' is how Zoot used to describe it. I remember the first time I went there thinking that Zoot was right, it *was* pictureskew (picturesque!! Must not get into habit of mispronouncing words) but at the same time being appalled, in my fearsome, only-child middle-classness, that people could actually 'live like that' —'like that' being Zoot, Zoot's parents, Zoot's two little brothers and one little sister, plus one squalling baby and a fractious grandmother all crammed cheek-by-jowl into a tiny fisherman's cottage.

'Imagine,' I remember saying to Abbey, as we cycled back together over the cobblestones, 'having to share a bedroom!'

'Some people don't even *have* bedrooms,' Abbey said. It was the sort of thing that Abbey was prone to say.

I remember going to David's, though not very often. It was such a long way out, it took nearly an hour, cycling. (From the middle of town, that was.) I remember Abbey's dad taking us once by car, when there was a party; and I remember one time when we did cycle, with me, as the shortest, using Abbey's little sister's bike so that Zoot, who hadn't got one, could use mine. I remember David being eager that we should learn horse-riding, and trying to give us lessons on Sable, his beautiful black gelding (a gelding is a castrated horse: I never knew that until David told me). I remember we all had a go, bumping round the paddock on the end of a leading rein, with David exhorting us to keep our heels up and our chins down (or was it

11

the other way round?) but we weren't of the stuff from which great riders were made. None of us really took to it, though Abbey did her best out of loyalty to David.

I remember that summer, the summer of the horse-riding. It was also the summer of the royal wedding —the one where Charles married Diana—and David and Abbey were already in the throes of becoming DavidnAbbey. I remember we all went to Brighton together for the day and on the train on the way back they sat and smooched and held hands (Zoot and I found it rather a trial, though later on we grew used to it and almost stopped noticing). I remember someone gave a royal wedding party at which David and Abbey disappeared and weren't found until a wandering parent tripped over them, in a huddle on the stairs. I remember—

So many things! So many, many things . . .

I remember David and Zoot, at the back of the assembly hall in morning assembly, piously dirging the words Catsmeat Potter Pirbright (they were going through a P.G. Wodehouse phase) to the tune of 'The Church's One Foundation', which was what the rest of us were singing. I remember the Great Rhetorical, sitting only centimetres away, turning a sort of mottled puce and making gobbling motions with his lips, and David and Zoot inclining their heads in reverence towards him and beaming at him as they dirged.

'Catsmeat Potter Pir*brigh*-hight
Catsmeat Potter Pir*bright*
Catsmeat Potter Pir*brigh*-hight
Catsmeat Potter Pir*bright*—'

What made it worse was that Zoot had just knocked out half a front tooth, falling off my bicycle. (He never did get that tooth capped: he still has a slight lisp even now.) I remember him falling off, it was because he was trying to impress us, going downhill without using his hands. He and David were always doing stupid things like that, but it always seemed to be Zoot who came to grief, never David. Zoot was the one who crashed bicycles, fell out of trees, chipped his teeth, broke his collar bone, knocked himself senseless on the side of the swimming pool. Accident-prone, that was Zoot. It was all too easy to imagine things happening to him; not to David.

I can remember why it was that Zoot was called Zoot. Some people have forgotten, or maybe never knew. They probably think it's because Zoot is a clownish sort of name and Zoot is a bit of a clownish sort of person. His real name is Thomas: Zoot suits him far better. It was David, actually, who christened him that. It was when we were all in the second year together, doing improvisations in French, and the only thing that Zoot could ever think of to say (him not being much gifted in the orating of foreign tongues) was, 'Zut alors!' He has been Zoot ever since.

Abbey, of course, is really Abigail. I am quite often shortened to Rob, or Robbie. David was the only one who was never shortened to anything. It's possible, I suppose, that when they were by themselves, in moments, as they say, of intimacy, Abbey may slurpily have murmured 'Davey' in his ear, but somehow I can't imagine it. David was essentially the one who *did* all the shortening and the nicknaming. For instance, there was a pop group around in those days (I don't think they exist any more) called The Shining White: David promptly re-named them The Whining Shite, and that is what we always knew them as. For a while, in our third year, he called me Bobbyn, which encouraged me to do a bit of fantasizing and dream

13

that maybe I was going to be The One—because we were all just a little bit in love with David—but it didn't mean anything. It was just his sense of humour. There wasn't ever anybody else; only Abbey.

When I say there wasn't anybody else, that's not strictly true: there was Max, as well. Max and David were inseparable, except when David was at school. They ate together (Max sitting on a chair at David's side), went out riding together, even slept together, with their heads together on the same pillow. Max is a smooth-haired fox terrier. He must be quite an old boy by now; about fifteen, I should think. I wonder if dogs have memories that stretch back like humans'?

It's strange, the things one's mind chooses to remember (as opposed to the myriad of things it chooses to forget). I remember, and I really can't think why, the day that Zoot's grandmother was buried. Zoot's grandmother didn't mean a thing to me, and I don't honestly think she meant all that much to Zoot, because she was a horrid, cantankerous old crone, but I remember the four of us, after Zoot had come back from the funeral, drinking coffee in a sea-front coffee bar and discussing how we should like *our* mortal remains disposed of when the time came. Zoot wanted to be thrown out to sea in a lobster pot with a note attached saying, *Food for sharks: human beings keep off.* I remember I opted for a full-scale burial service, with loads of flowers and incense and priests intoning liturgies, or whatever it is they intone, and requiem masses being sung for the repose of my soul. I remember Abbey saying that that was nauseating, and her and David both agreeing that the one thing they did *not* want was 'any of that religious stuff'. Abbey said that she would like a humanist ceremony, and David said that when Max died he would bury him in his

14

favourite corner of the garden and plant a bush over him in memory, and there wouldn't be any cant or hypocrisy, just a simple honest farewell, because when you were dead you were dead and no amount of mumbo jumbo was going to bring you back and as far as he was concerned religion was just one great con trick.

That was another reason that the Great Rhetorical had it in for David. Being our official RI indoctrinator, he naturally felt pretty strongly on the subject, not liking it to be dismissed as mumbo jumbo or some kind of con trick. He once gave David zilch out of a hundred for an RI exam and wrote at the bottom, *Did you really hope to get away with this?* Ever since the Catsmeat incident he had held that David was a corrupting influence, especially over Abbey. He really thought that if it weren't for David and his irreverent attitude Abbey would be a model of piety, humility and religious fervour. He couldn't have been more wrong. If anything, it was the other way round and Abbey who influenced David—Abbey who influenced *all* of us.

In spite of her seeming docility, Abbey actually has a very strong streak of obstinacy in her, she certainly won't be pushed around, and while she doesn't exactly push others around she nonetheless has a most decided knack of imposing her will when it comes to matters of what you might call principle. Abbey is a great one for principles. She is also a great one for *organizing*, and for setting things in motion. It was Abbey, for example, who nagged us all into joining Greenpeace and CND and writing to our MPs. It wasn't that we weren't every bit as concerned as she was about nuclear accidents and pollution and germ warfare, every bit as outraged at the obscenities being perpetrated in our name while we just sat around and

15

did nothing, but without Abbey to keep on at us and prod at our consciences we would most likely just have gone on sitting around, gone on doing nothing. As it was, she marshalled us, got us all out there waving our banners and going on demos. David and Zoot, of course, being men and feeling that their precious masculinity was at stake, used to take the mickey — 'Yes, miss, no, miss, three bags full, miss!' 'Rap our knuckles, change our nappies, smack our botties, ooh, lovely!'—but it was only show. They always went along with her in the end.

I remember once when David and Zoot were discussing whether we should go to a party being given by someone in the Sixth, where, so rumour had it, pot was going to be freely available. None of us had ever smoked pot. (Some of us still haven't. *I* haven't, and I'm pretty sure that Abbey hasn't. Zoot probably has.) I remember that David and Zoot were eager to try, they kept urging us to 'come along' and 'give it a whirl' and 'let our hair down for once'. I remember that I was tempted. I might well have been swayed—but for Abbey putting her foot down.

I remember she'd been listening as we talked and quite suddenly she erupted and let forth this furious diatribe. What did people need drugs for? Weren't there enough other things in life? Books, and music, and dancing, and—

'Sex?'

'Sex!'

'Smackie bottie—'

'Ooh, lovely!'

They just couldn't resist it. But they couldn't resist Abbey, either. She won the day, just as she always did. We never went to the party: we never took pot. Instead, I remember, we all gathered at my place and had a party of our own, just the four of us. DavidnAbbey, Robyn and Zoot . . . a unit; complete. We almost didn't need other people. I remember the Great Rhetorical asking sarkily why we didn't set up a commune, and old Willie Wilkins whingeing at Abbey that 'you live too much in each other's pockets'. We didn't take any notice of Willie, any more than we did of the Windbag. Why should we? It was fun, being us.

It was fun, I remember, the day that we went to Brighton (the day when DavidnAbbey smooched all the way home). I remember we had our fortunes told by a so-called gypsy sitting in a beach hut with a crystal ball made of plastic. The fortunes were terribly cryptic. Zoot's was 'Seek and ye shall find', Abbey's was 'Look to the end of the rainbow', mine was 'Ride the big horses', which I took to be an allusion to my career as an actress but which David said went to show that I should have persisted with the riding lessons while I still had the opportunity. He wouldn't tell us what his fortune was (David could be funny like that: there were times when he closed in on himself and became almost secretive) and I remember that Zoot and I amused ourselves trying to guess. I remember Zoot came up with 'Beware the galloping knob rot!' and that I suggested 'Look to your rear'. We thought it highly amusing. David just smiled in a superior fashion and informed us that little things, etc. Abbey said, 'Oh, for*get* the stupid fortunes! Let's go on the dodgems.' So we did, and spent our time crashing into each other.

I remember that day at Brighton, and I remember another day, too, on our own beach at Clearhaven. I remember us all lounging there, David throwing stones for Max, Zoot and Abbey trying to get a sun tan, me trying *not* to get a sun tan (on account of sun

17

bringing me out in blotches) and Pilch Maguire and Andy Dove coming towards us over the horizon. I remember that Pilch (who was always tremendously butch) was wearing a pair of very tight, very faded blue jeans, slung low down on his hips with the crutch all bursting out.

'Cor, sexy!' I said.

I remember Zoot lazily rolling over to look, and Andy, growing self-conscious, even though it wasn't him that was being looked at, doing a little hoppity-skip to catch up with Pilch. I remember Zoot, very softly, under his breath, starting up the Andy Pandy song: 'Andy Pandy's coming to play . . .'

'Tra-la-la la la-la!'

I remember giggling (being of the age to giggle) as David joined in, and poor old Andy scuttling off like a frightened crab in the wake of Pilch (who couldn't have cared less, or so he made out). I remember the song continuing—'Andy Pandy's ever so gay, Tra-la-la la la-la!'—and Abbey, from her prone position, face down in the sand, muttering, 'Shut up!' which instantly set David and Zoot off on their mickey-taking.

'Shut up! Shut up!'

'Who's a naughty boy?'

'Smackie bottie—'

'Ooh, lovely!'

I remember Abbey sitting up and snapping, 'Look, will you just stop being so beastly!' and the inane chorus of 'Beastly, beastly!' and Abbey at that growing really mad and demanding to know how *they* would like it; and Zoot cackling and wringing his hands, and David, being flip, as he chucked another stone for Max, airily dismissing Pilch and Andy as 'just another couple of poofs'. Goodness, how furious Abbey was!

18

She was quite right, of course, and they *knew* she was quite right, it wasn't as if they really had it in for gays, they just couldn't stop themselves, all the silly he-man stuff, it was even more pathetic than Pilch doing his butch bit. They took it quite well, Abbey having a go at them; it was Abbey who refused to be mollified. She said she'd never heard anything so childish and so stupid.

'It's not only stupid, it's prejudiced. It's bigoted. It's—'

I can't remember what else it was. I think it must have been at that point that David hurled himself at her and started a wrestling match, which needless to say very speedily turned into something quite different, with me and Zoot pretending not to notice and Max going berserk and digging a trench right round the pair of them, front paws going like steam hammers, in a frenzied bid for attention—which of course he got in the end. He always did. You can't ignore a really determined fox terrier. Pretty soon Zoot and I had started to help him with his trenches until finally we'd dug such a big hole that David and Abbey rolled over the edge and fell in; whereupon we promptly buried them in the sand and sat upon them . . .

Oh! Those were the golden days, those days that I remember. And David—David was the golden boy. It seemed then as if the sun would shine on him for ever.

2

I remember the day, a day towards the end of the spring term of our sixth year, when David came into school limping and looking rather sheepish. It was a Monday, I remember. I remember it quite clearly, because on the Sunday Abbey and I had gone on a march and Abbey had been incensed because both David and Zoot had made excuses for not joining us. Zoot's excuse had been that he had to give his father a hand to mend the roof: David's that he had some reading to catch up on. You couldn't really argue in Zoot's case because at least it was genuine work; in David's we tended to be sceptical, for while it was perfectly true that David always had to slog that little bit harder than Abbey, who is just naturally mad clever, I know we both suspected that what he really wanted to do was spend the day out riding, with Sable and with Max.

I remember him that morning, making his way towards us across the common room, and Zoot, not exactly gloating but with just a slight edge of triumph to his voice, yelling, 'Hey! I thought I was the one that was going to fall off the roof?' (because if anyone would, it would be Zoot) and Abbey demanding to know, 'What have you *done*?' And I remember David giving a sort of half grin, a mixture of shamefacedness and bravado, and saying that he'd gone out for a ride (Abbey turned and looked at me: we both of us rolled our eyes) and that Sable had taken a corner a bit too sharply in the woods and crushed his leg against a tree. He added quickly that it wasn't Sable's fault.

'Well, of course it wasn't!' said Abbey. 'If you'd performed your public duty as you should have done and come on the march with us you wouldn't have *been* in the woods in the first place.'

Zoot was just worried about David being unable to play football: 'We've got that match against Joseph's on Friday.'

'Oh, I'll be all right for that,' said David. 'It's only a bruise.'

I remember the match against St Joseph's. It was a freezing cold day, dripping with rain, and Abbey and me like a couple of goons standing on the sidelines, cheering. David played even though his leg was black and blue and twice the size of normal, but shortly before the end of the first half some hulk of a full-back barged into him and must have hacked him on the shin because the next thing we knew he was rolling about in hoops and having to be helped off.

'I see that Abbey's young man has been in the wars,' Pop said, when he got back home from surgery that evening. (He always referred to David as 'Abbey's young man'. It used to irk me in the early days, when I still cherished secret daydreams, but by the time we'd reached our sixth year I'd accepted the daydreams for what they were. I'd learnt to live with the fact of DavidnAbbey: it didn't torment me any more.)

'Did he come and see you?' I said. 'Some lout went and kicked him.'

'Well, they certainly did a good job . . . that's a bruise that will be there for a week or two.'

I remember, after that, it was the Easter holidays. I remember the weather turned overnight from being rainy and bleak to being absolutely glorious, and we lay on the beach and watched David's leg turn from black-and-blue to deepest purple and then, very

21

slowly, back through the spectrum—mauve, yellow, yellowy-brown, beige—until it was almost normal again. The trouble was that even though it was normal in colour it was far from normal in size. It was still swollen and painful, which meant that we had no alternative but to be lazy, which suited me because I was reading Chekhov plays (I had vowed to read the lot before the end of the holidays) but didn't suit the other two at all. Zoot kept agitating about cricket and the coming season. The first match was only weeks away; how was David going to get his eye in if he couldn't practise? How was *Zoot* going to get his eye in if David couldn't practise? Abbey said that he ought to go back to the doctor (i.e., Pop or Dr Dearmont). She said it was ridiculous, letting it drag on like this. Suppose a bit of bone had got cracked? He could end up crippled for life.

'Isn't that so?' She turned, almost aggressively, on me, seeking confirmation. 'Shouldn't you get these things looked at?'

'I suppose so,' I said. (I was busy being Masha, at the time, from *The Three Sisters*: my thoughts were all full of going to Moscow.)

'I mean, don't *you* think he ought to go back?'

'Mm,' I said. (*My dear sisters, I've got something to confess to you . . .*) 'Probably.'

'The longer you leave things, the longer they take to get better. Especially bones. They can get permanently deformed. Can't they?'

Abbey poked at me, crossly. *This is serious: stop your play-acting and give me your support!* Reluctantly I abandoned Masha and sat up.

'They can,' I said, since that was obviously what she wanted. People always expect me to know about these things, what with Pop being a GP, but in fact I've never been the slightest bit interested. If anything, I've tended to keep very well clear. Abbey used to like nothing better, when she was going through her doctor phase, than to come round to our house and help herself to one of Pop's medical tomes. She used to spend hours absolutely enthralled, boning up on General Paralysis of the Insane or Huntington's Chorea. Not me. I've always thought it just a touch morbid. Not very *nice*. (Abbey would probably say, even now, that 'It's best to know rather than remain in ignorance.' She always believes in confronting things head-on, does Abbey.)

Anyway, she nagged and nagged at us, until I was forced to come out positively and say yes, it *was* always best to be on the safe side, and yes, that *was* what doctors were for, and yes, it *was* what we all paid into the NHS for, and yes, we *should* all get our money's worth, and yes *of course* Pop would agree with me; and David, finally, goaded into making some sort of commitment, saying all right, then, maybe, perhaps next week or the week after, at any rate he would think about it, and if it didn't get any better—

'Then you'll go,' said Abbey.

David said yes, he would go.

It seemed after that, in fact, that it did start to get a bit better, or maybe he was just pretending because of not wanting to have to go to the bother of queuing up in the surgery for hours (and who should blame him? I can't *stand* it. You'd think the least they could do is have a proper appointments system) but at any rate he left off using a stick to hobble around with and didn't seem to be limping quite so badly, and actually tried playing a bit of cricket on the beach one morning. He couldn't bowl, but that didn't really matter because Zoot is the bowler, David was what is known as a stylish opening bat, and that morning he was stylish to some purpose, driving no less than three balls over the breakwater and out to sea for six. (But naturally couldn't retrieve them: Max and I had to do that.)

When we started back to school for the summer term he was still perceptibly limping—the Great Rhetorical, with whom we had been cursed for a second time round as class teacher, took much pleasure in referring to him as the Walking Wounded —but his name was down for the cricket Eleven, he auditioned with me for the end-of-term play (*Much Ado About Nothing*: I aimed for the part of Beatrice, no less) and opted with the rest of us to join the fencing class. He had never made any mention of having gone back to see Pop, and Pop had never said anything —though of course he wouldn't, necessarily: secrets of the surgery and all that—so we were all taken by surprise when on the first Friday of term he casually announced that he couldn't attend some cruddy lunch-time debate the Great Rhetorical had organized as he had an appointment at the hospital.

The Great Rhetorical took it as practically a personal insult. Anyone would have thought, the way he carried on, that David had arranged the appointment on purpose to clash. Nor was the Windbag the only one to be put out: Abbey was pretty indignant, too. Zoot and I weren't so much indignant as curious. We waited till we got him outside, at break, then bombarded him.

'Why didn't you *tell* us?' (That was Abbey; rightly feeling spurned.)

'Didn't think.'

'Didn't *think*?'

'Well . . . it didn't seem that important.'

'So who are you going to see?' (That was me, taking

a professional interest.)

'I dunno. Some specialist.'

'Which one?'

'Can't remember.'

'Mr Grainger's the fracture man.' I knew about Mr Grainger because he was a friend of Pop's. 'Is it Mr Grainger?'

'Don't think so.'

'So what's he a specialist *in*?'

'Dunno.'

'Bones?'

'Could be.'

'If it was bones it'd be Mr—'

'Oh, shut up, Robyn! Keeping on! What did Robyn's dad say?'

'Didn't see Robyn's dad. Saw the other one.'

'Dr Dearmont? He's nice! He's—'

'Oh, do shut *up*, Robyn! What did Dr Dearmont say?'

'Didn't say anything.'

'He must have said *some*thing!'

'Just said to go and have it looked at.'

'Well, I hope you're going to be back in time for the meeting.'

'What meeting?'

'CND!' It was Abbey's aim to set up a sub-branch at school. 'Don't say you'd forgotten?'

'Oh, that!' said David. 'No, of course I hadn't.'

It was obvious that he had. There were times when he and Zoot really could be awfully cavalier towards poor old Abbey. She'd been going on about her wretched meeting all through the holidays. They knew how much it meant to her.

'Sorry,' said David, not really sounding it. 'I'll get back if I can.'

25

'You'd better,' said Abbey. 'Anyway,'—she fixed her attention, Medusa-like, upon me and Zoot—'you two'll be there.'

It wasn't so much a question as a statement: not so much a statement as a threat. Zoot and I both opened our mouths at the same time.

'Er—'

'After you,' I said, smartly.

'Thing is,' said Zoot, 'I'm down for nets. Four till six-thirty. Barney'll do his nut if I'm not there.'

Silence. David began massaging his leg. I scraped with my teeth at the remnants of last week's nail polish.

'Are you telling me,' said Abbey, 'that a paltry game of cricket is of more importance than the future of mankind?'

'I'm not,' said Zoot. 'It's Barney. Naturally, if it was up to me—'

Naturally, if it was up to Zoot he would trot along to his net practice and let the future of mankind go hang. Abbey turned, contemptuously, from Zoot to me.

'Well, at least *Robyn*—'

'I'll certainly come if I feel up to it,' I said.

'What do you mean, *if you feel up to it*?'

'If I'm not prostrate with agony.'

'Why should you be prostrate with agony?'

'I think I might be coming on.'

'Oh, for heaven's sake!' Abbey tossed her hair back over her shoulders. (David and Zoot exchanged grimaces: she's off again . . .) 'This becomes ludicrous, every month! Why can't you go on the pill, or something?'

'I don't want to go on the pill. It gives you blood clots.'

'Of course it doesn't!'

'Sometimes it does.'

'Only if you smoke.'

'I don't care, I don't fancy the idea.'

'And anyway,' said Zoot, 'only bad girls go on the pill . . . Robyn's not a bad girl, are you?' He leered at me, in that silly way men have when they think they're being sexy. 'Robyn's a *good* girl. Robyn doesn't *need* to go on the pill. Robyn wouldn't—'

'Yes, and you can shut up!' said Abbey.

'Oh, charming! Thank you very much!'

'Such a lady.'

'Lady smack a wristie?'

'Lady smack a bot-bot?'

'Ooh, lovely!'

Abbey ignored them.

'It's just stupid, month after month—specially with your father being a doctor, for goodness' sake!'

'Doesn't make any difference. He might just as well be a coal miner. *He* won't do anything . . . he makes me go along to the surgery same as everyone else.'

'Well, go, then!'

'That's right,' said David. 'Flog us all into hypochondria.'

Abbey turned on him.

'I was right to make you go, wasn't I? They wouldn't be sending you to a specialist if they didn't think it needed looking at.'

'Housemaid's knee,' said David.

'It's a very funny place,' said Abbey, witheringly, 'to have housemaid's knee!'

'Well, shin, then . . . housemaid's shin.'

'It obviously still needs looking at.'

'Before it turns gangrenous,' said Zoot, 'and has to be took off.'

'Will you just shut *up*?' said Abbey. 'And you'—she

27

swung back, venomously, to me—'go and get something *done*. If you won't go on the pill, then get some tablets or something. *Any*thing. So long as it stops you moaning.'

'I don't moan! And anyway, I don't approve of all this tablet-taking. People these days,' I said, 'treat doctors like dispensing machines . . . penny in the slot and a bottle of pills. In the old days they just used to put up with things.'

'In the old days,' said Abbey, 'they used to *die* of things.'

'Well, I still don't think one ought to go running off to one's GP just for every least little ache and pain.'

I shouldn't have said that: I stepped right into it.

'If it's only a little ache and pain,' snapped Abbey, 'then you can jolly well make an effort and come along to the meeting!'

I did go to the meeting (David didn't make it). I went out of loyalty to Abbey more than anything else. I was still having Omnious Rumblings but they weren't yet actually unbearable, so although I could have thought of better ways of spending my time, such as starting to learn the part of Beatrice (just in case) it would have seemed a bit churlish, leaving poor old Abbey to get on with it by herself. So I went along and did my duty, and stood at Abbey's side and supported the cause, and in fact we did quite well, we collected over thirty signatures, and everybody who signed promised faithfully to come to the next local CND meeting (about ten of them actually did: two of them even *joined*) so as Abbey said, it certainly wasn't a wasted evening.

The next day, however, which of course was Saturday, and supposed to be a day for enjoying oneself, I woke up with more than just Omnious Rumblings, I woke up with Positive Gripes, and I thought that Abbey was quite right (when is she not?), it *was* ludicrous, carrying on like this. It was becoming a nuisance: it was becoming *tiresome*. After lunch we were driving over to Winchester to spend the night with Gran and Grandad, and that evening we were going to the theatre to see *The Three Sisters*, which is one of my most favourite of plays (Masha being one of my most favourite of parts, second only to Beatrice). How could I concentrate on Chekhov if I were being racked in vilest agony?

At breakfast, very loudly and pointedly, addressing myself to the marmalade jar, I said: 'I've got the guts ache.'

'Oh, dear, not again?' said Mumps. (The reason I call her Mumps is that when I was small she used to call me Pumpkin, shortened to Pumps. She became Mumpkin, shortened, etc. Mumps stuck: Pumps, I'm glad to say, did not.) 'This is getting to be a habit! What are we going to do about it?'

'Aspirin,' said Pop, behind his newspaper.

I gritted my teeth. (We had been through this before.)

'Aspirin does not work.'

'So ask the chemist for something.'

'I have. *Nothing* works.'

Pop lowered his newspaper—not to talk to me, simply to locate his coffee cup.

'In that case, I can only suggest you go to see a doctor . . . preferably within working hours. I am happy to say'—he clawed his cup towards him —'that I personally am not on duty this morning.'

I wonder whether people that have solicitors for fathers are told to 'go and see a solicitor' every time they just want to sue someone? It's all very unsatisfactory, if you ask me.

I was surprised, when I got to the surgery (where of course, it being Saturday, there was only the one partner on and a queue about ninety deep) to find David there. His mother was with him, which struck me as odd, since David was never the sort to tote his mother around. I thought he looked a bit uncomfortable as I came marching in, and I thought that that was probably why. And then I thought that maybe having housemaid's shin meant that he couldn't drive (he usually borrowed one of the family cars, usually the Land Rover) and that to save him having to drag in on the bus Mrs Geary had driven him in herself.

She's very beautiful, David's mother; very beautiful, and rather remote. We've never got to know her the way I know Abbey's mum and Abbey knows mine and we both of us know Zoot's. I suppose, really, it's because we haven't seen as much of her. She smiled at me that morning, just a slight curve of the lips, but didn't say hallo or anything. I thought probably it was the effect of being in a doctor's waiting room. It gets some people like that; as if it's a place of worship where even just normal breathing is an act of desecration. I've never had those sort of qualms. I think waiting rooms should be jolly and full of the buzz of interesting conversation.

'So how's the housemaid's?' I said to David.

'Still housemaiding. What are you doing here?'

'Me? Oh, I've just come to pass the time of day . . . I *like* sitting around in doctors' waiting rooms. Much more fun than being handed a prescription across the breakfast table by one's own father, who can't be bothered because *we're not on duty* this morning . . . it's Dr Dearmont. Not that I *mind* seeing Dr Dearmont,

30

it's just that it's all such a stupid waste of time.'

'You can say that again!'

David spoke with some feeling. I suddenly remembered: 'How did your hospital thing go?'

'All right.'

'What happened? Did they keep you hanging around for hours?'

'Only most of the afternoon.'

'Doing what?'

'Oh . . . this and that. You know what they're like.'

'So what did they—'

The buzzer at this point went and buzzed for the next patient, which was David, so I never got round to asking him what they had said. Mrs Geary was already over at the door, waiting. (She was actually going to go *in* with him. I remember thinking that I wouldn't want my mother coming in with me. Most offputting.) David stood up, and melodramatically raised a hand.

'*Morituri te salutamus.*'

'You what?' I said. I never did Latin. I couldn't see any point in it.

'*Morituri—*'

'David!'

David pulled a face.

'See you Monday,' I said.

3

David wasn't there on Monday. I bumped into Abbey at the school gates and she was all by herself. I said, 'Where's David?' (because they always used to meet up at the bus stop and walk in together—*holding hands*).

'He's in hospital,' said Abbey.

I said, 'Hospital?' in that silly, parrot-like way that one does when something takes one by surprise. 'What's he in hospital for?'

'They said he'd got to.'

'What, for his leg?' (What else? *Stupid* questions one asks.) 'I only saw him on Saturday!'

'Yes, I know; he said.'

'So when did they—'

'Sunday.'

'Wow!' They certainly can move with the speed of greased lightning when they feel like it. Pop's known people who've been on the waiting list till the day they died. 'How long's he going to be in?'

'Don't know; they didn't say.'

'I don't expect it'll be long. They like to push them out pretty quickly . . . shortage of beds and all that.'

'I just hope it's not going to keep him laid up for ages. I've got that rounders match organized for half-term.'

The rounders match—girls versus boys—was another of Abbey's brainchilds. We always used to have a special midsummer fête at Clareville in aid of charity (Guild Day, it was called) and the mixed rounders was going to be one of that year's major attractions, with people sponsoring us, so much per rounder, plus of course a collection at the end. Not without good reason, Abbey was counting on David as being her star turn: the main puller-in of loot.

'Bones are such a bore,' she said. 'They take for ever.'

'Have they got to put him in plaster?'

'He doesn't seem to know. He just said they wanted him in.'

'So who did he see? Did he see Mr Grainger?'

'What *is* all this with Mr Grainger?' Abbey turned on me, accusingly. 'Have you got a thing about him, or what?'

'I was just trying to find out, that's all. I mean, if it's a fracture—'

'How long would it take?'

'Month? Six weeks?'

'As long as that?'

I didn't really know—never having fractured myself.

'I'll ask Pop,' I said.

We walked on, through the gates.

'Funny, them not saying how long he'd have to be in.'

'Why?' Abbey's head switched back again, sharply. 'What's funny about it?'

'Well . . . I'd've thought they would.'

'Perhaps they did and he didn't remember. He was more bothered about the animals than anything else . . . having to be away from them.'

'Let it be a lesson to him,' I said. 'That's what comes of people going riding when they ought to be out marching . . . they get their legs crushed against trees. And serve them right,' I prompted; but for once Abbey seemed disinclined to take up the theme. She only

33

shook her head, rather abstractedly, and said, 'Mm.'

'Anyway, *I'll* be all right,' I told her. I thought that at least would cheer her up. (She was an awful wet blanket when David was away.) 'I went to the doctor's Saturday and he gave me these tablets. They're fantastic! I told you we were going to Winchester, didn't I? To see my grandparents? Well, we went to the theatre . . . *Three Sisters*. It was lousy, actually. The girl playing Masha was absolutely *dire*. And everyone kept going round being all deep and gloomy. I mean, it's meant to be a comedy, for heaven's sake! The only time anyone laughed was when Protopopov got his foot caught under the sofa and nearly dragged it off stage with him . . . I mean, people were just falling asleep, practically. This old man in the row behind suddenly started snoring, and his wife had to wake him up, and he said, "Oh, God! Is it still going on?" and everyone just about collapsed . . . but anyway, *normally*, me being in that state, I'd've been in such ghastly awful agony I'd've never managed to sit through it, I'd probably have gone out and been sick or something, but with these tablets that he gave me I just didn't feel a thing, they're an absolute knock-out . . . so even if half-term—' I sidestepped a flying tennis ball—'even if half-term does come at the wrong time, which it very well might, it won't matter, because all I have to do is take a couple of these tablets and I won't even know what's happening.'

'That's good,' said Abbey, forging ahead.

I did a little leap to catch up with her.

'I thought you'd be interested,' I said. I'd known she wouldn't care two straws for Chekhov, but I did think she'd have shown a bit more enthusiasm about me having got my guts problem sorted out, considering she was the one that had nagged me into it. 'I thought you'd be pleased,' I said.

'I told you,' said Abbey. 'You should have done it ages ago.'

That was all I could get out of her—'you should have done it ages ago.' She was in a most peculiar and unAbbey-like mood. Because of David, no doubt. They were like a couple of moon calves, those two: separate them for only five minutes and they started to droop. If that was what love did for you, then heaven preserve me! Somewhat disgruntled, I took myself off to look for Zoot, instead. Not that he was any more interested in Chekhov than Abbey, but at least the story of the old man amused him. He said it might be rather fun, when David was back, if we were to pull a similar stunt in the middle of one of the Great Rhetorical's windbaggy lectures. We could draw lots for which of us was going to be the snorer.

'Abbey wouldn't do it,' I said.

'Oh, well! Abbey.'

He didn't say it unkindly; it was just that Abbey never fooled about like the rest of us did. She wasn't a goody goody, only rather solemn. She was specially solemn all the rest of that day. She seemed preoccupied, in a world of her own—she even had a run-in with Willie for not paying attention in one of her chemistry classes. This was something that was reported to me by Zoot (me having given up chemistry, or chemistry having given up me, way back in the fourth year). The fact that he found it significant enough to mention shows how unusual it was, how untypical of Abbey.

It never occurred to me until much later that she might actually have been worried about David. Nobody had worried about Zoot when he had gone into hospital with his collar bone. Of course, a collar

35

bone wasn't the same as a leg, but then Zoot had actually broken things, he had actually smashed himself up. David obviously couldn't have done that much damage or he wouldn't even have been able to hobble. Perhaps a hairline fracture of the fibula —fibia? tibula? Well, whatever it was—the little stick-like bone that joins the knee part to the ankle. It was a nuisance, that was all. It would be specially a nuisance if it meant him missing out on the rounders match.

I asked Pop about it that evening.

'How long does it take for a fracture to heal?'

'Depends what sort of fracture.'

'The sort of fracture David might have.'

I remember Pop frowning: he doesn't encourage gossip about patients.

'We don't yet *know* what sort of fracture David might have.'

'Well, then, legs . . . in general.'

'I cannot possibly commit myself to legs in general.'

I sighed. It's always hard going with these professional types. You can never ask them a simple question and get given a simple answer.

'What I want to know is, will he be OK for playing rounders at half-term?' If I could just set Abbey's mind at rest on that one particular point. 'We have this very important match. It's for charity . . . we really need to know if he's going to be OK. I mean, he won't have to be in plaster or anything?'

Pop spread his hands.

'Am I the Almighty? Or am I just a humble GP?'

He may have been just a GP; humble is hardly an adjective I would have applied to him. In my experience, doctors as a race are far from humble.

'You could at least hazard a guess,' I said.

Pop assumed one of his lordly expressions (he has a

range): 'I am not in the business of guessing.'

'And anyway'—Mumps said it gently, but nonetheless firmly—'you know he can't discuss patients with you.'

'It's not patients,' I said, 'it's David.'

'Don't be obtuse,' said Pop.

Mumps said, 'David or not, he's still a patient.'

She might just as well have added, *so run along, now, there's a good girl*. The message came across, loud and clear: doctors' little daughters should be seen and not heard . . .

I gave up.

'And when, pray'—the Great Rhetorical peered at us over the tops of his spectacles (sheer affectation: he had to hoist his eyebrows right up into his hairline and practically quadruple his chins before he could do it)—'when, pray, may we expect the Walking Wounded to come amongst us again?'

He addressed the question impartially to the three of us, Zoot and Abbey and me. Zoot and I turned, automatically, to Abbey.

'We don't yet know,' she said.

She said it somewhat stonily. The Windbag had made the inquiry in his usual sarky tones, obviously striving for effect and not really giving a damn. Worse, he had even sounded a touch exultant: the enemy had taken a tumble, and he could hardly contain his gleefulness and mirth. It was naturally very irksome to Abbey. She had spoken to David's mother the night before, but hadn't been able to glean very much; only that they were 'still doing tests'. I suppose it made her a bit anxious.

'One imagines'—the Windbag threw up his arms, rhapsodically—'that this is how Rome must have been without Caesar—the cinema without Rudolf Valentino—'

Someone said, 'Rudolf who?'

'Who's Rudolf Valentino?'

A faint glimmer crossed the Windbag's pudding-like features: he doesn't care for interruptions when he's in the middle of his rhetoricals.

'—a church without a figurehead—a throne without the king—'

('I think he's talking about Elvis Presley.')

'—really, it's a wonder the school still functions!'

'It doesn't,' said Zoot. 'We just lost to Manor House by eight wickets.'

Laughter; against the Windbag. This time something more than a faint glimmer crossed his features: this time it was a spasm of what looked almost like loathing. And in that instant I suddenly realized something. I suddenly realized what the Windbag's problem was: he was jealous. It had never crossed my mind before, because in general such things don't, but in that one brief flash I saw it quite clearly. He was actually jealous—of David! Of his youth, I suppose, and the fact of his being so well liked. And now he was in hospital, and it was the Windbag's little moment of triumph: the moment to gloat. He really was a creep.

On Wednesday Abbey said, 'I'm going to visit David this evening. Do you want to come with me?' She seemed very eager for me and Zoot to go with her. I remember thinking that if I were Abbey and deep in love I should want to go by myself, I wouldn't want to have to share David with other people, but I believe she must have been a bit nervous about the hospital environment because when I said, 'What, both of us? Will they let us all in?' she said, 'We'll just *go* in.' It wasn't like Abbey to be defiant in the face of authority, so I guessed she must be feeling the need of moral support.

We arranged to meet Zoot at the main entrance to the hospital at seven o'clock, and in the meanwhile I rang home to say that I'd be going back to Abbey's for tea. (It's a longish journey from Parkmead, which is where my parents live, into the centre of town. Parkmead in fact is about five miles from Mailoo Farm, which is way out in the grasslands, real cowpat stuff.)

Sophie was there at tea-time. Sophie is Abbey's sister. She's four years younger than Abbey and me, and so of course we have always thought of her as quite a baby. (She was in her second year when we were in our sixth: now she's in the sixth herself.) Being a baby didn't stop her having a thing about David. Most of the second year (female division) had a thing about David. I think it was Sophie who probably started it, and the rest just followed suit. It had become somewhat of a cult—which of course was another reason for the Great Rhetorical being jealous. If anyone was going to be a cult figure, then it ought to be him . . . some hopes!

Sophie had designed a special good luck card in her art class that morning. I *think* it was supposed to be a black cat with a bow round its neck (it actually looked like a small squat Chinaman without any feet). Inside it she had written, 'With love from Sophie, XXXXXXXXXXXXXXXX.' She entrusted it to me, 'because Abbey's so absent-minded,' and made me promise 'not to forget to give it to him, will you?' I promised that I wouldn't.

Out of deference to me, stuck with boring school gear (we didn't actually have to wear uniforms once we'd reached the sixth, but we were expected to be reasonably wholesome) Abbey said at first that she'd stay as she was. I told her, however, that she owed it to David to put something decent on. I had the feeling she was quite glad to be persuaded. Abbey isn't what you'd call fashion crazy, but she does care about clothes—more than I do, really, which is odd, considering that I'm the theatrical one and she's the scientist. Left to myself I'll throw on the first thing that comes to hand, anything so long as it's *bright*, but Abbey actually considers the occasion and chooses. That night she chose a white cotton top and tight white pants which showed off her legs and her bum. Abbey's legs are very long and slender, and her bum is enviably small. (Mine tends to balloon, rather. Zoot, the pig, whenever I wore trousers, used to say that it looked like 'two ferrets fighting in a bag'.)

David was in something called the Humphrey Spencer Ward, which was situated on the ground floor in the annexe, looking out across the flower beds and lawns. Quite reasonable, as hospital wards go. It was all divided up into glass-partitioned cubicles, four beds to a cubicle, much more modern than the wards in the main building, which are long and cavernous and have beds arranged in rows down each side, like hangovers from the Crimean War.

There weren't any notices saying only two visitors at a time and nobody stopped us as we walked in. David was right down at the far end (I tried not to be nosy and peer into all the other cubicles as we passed). He was sitting up in bed, looking relatively cheerful and wearing red pyjamas. I remember thinking, 'This is the first time I have ever seen David in pyjamas . . . ' Some big deal! There's no denying, however, that clothes—lack of clothes, inappropriate clothes—do change a person's image. Not that pyjamas could be considered inappropriate as *such*, given the circumstances, but I suppose it was the very fact of those circumstances, of David being in bed, us being there seeing him in bed, which struck me as wrong. Like peering through a lighted window watching someone undress, or spying on them when they're asleep.

It took me several minutes to shake it off, this sensation of things not being as they ought to be. (Of David no longer being David? Being diminished, being reduced in status?) I think Abbey must have experienced something of the same, for just at the beginning she was even more awkward than I was. It was fortunate that Zoot was there: he can always be depended upon to plough ahead regardless. By the time he had finished going through the Manor Park fiasco in ball-by-ball detail (employing language which I can only describe as colourful) Abbey and I had managed to pull ourselves together.

'Look,' I said to David. 'Sophie made a card for you.'

'Ooh, lovely!' said David. 'What is it?'

'Big furry arse,' said Zoot.

'It's a good luck card, you idiot!'

'It's a haggis,' said David.

'It's not a haggis! It's a cat.'

'Looks like a haggis to me.'

'Well, it's not! Don't be so mean. She did it for you specially—you ought to be flattered.'

'I am flattered . . . I'm extremely flattered someone should send me a haggis! I shall put it on my locker and dream of it at night.'

'What's it like in here at night? Is it creepy?'

'You wanna bet?' Zoot hunched himself up, making creeping motions with his fingers. 'All that luscious female flesh just five yards down the corridor . . . '

'All that luscious female flesh happens to be the geriatric ward,' said David.

'Hah!' Abbey flashed a triumphant look at Zoot: not so clever after all . . .

'So what's this one?' I said.

'This what?'

'This ward.'

'Humphrey Spencer.'

'No, I mean . . . what's it for?' David looked blank. 'Orthopaedic?'

'What's orthopaedic?' said Zoot.

'Bones.'

'I thought paedics was children?'

'Well, he is a child, I expect . . . medically speaking.'

'He can't be,' said Abbey. She lowered her voice. 'There's some quite old men in here.'

'Geriatrics!' yelled Zoot.

Abbey threw a punch at him.

'*Quiet!* Do you want to get us chucked out?'

They didn't chuck us out, even though the double act started up and at times became a bit noisy (at times a bit *bawdy*). It actually turned into quite a fun visit, though David didn't seem to have any idea when they were likely to let him out. He said they were still at the stage of prodding and poking and taking pretty pictures, trying to decide on the best course of action.

I said, 'So who are you under? Mr Grainger?' and everybody groaned. They were all convinced that I had a thing about him. It wasn't that at all. It was just that I knew that he was bones.

Next day the results of the audition for *Much Ado* were announced . . . David had been cast as Benedick, I was down for Beatrice. The first thing I did on reading the cast list was look for Abbey to tell her the news. I knew she'd be glad about David, even though she herself had no ambitions that way. It would have taken a whole herd of wild horses to have dragged Abbey up on stage. Still, I did think that maybe, knowing the rest of us were going to be involved (Zoot had got the part of Dogberry, the pompous policeman) she might be prevailed upon to offer her services as stage management. It was always far more fun if we did things together.

'Where's Abbey?' I said, snatching at Avril Ellison as she came out of the science lab.

'Willie asked her to stay behind.'

'Oh.' I pulled a face. If Willie was jawing at her, she'd be there for the rest of break.

Miss Wilkins was senior science. She and I had had a hate thing going ever since the second year, when she apostrophized me as a repulsive little glutton just because she'd caught me crouched behind the back bench in the lab consuming jam doughnuts. She also said that I was a bad influence on Abbey. Strange how people were for ever accusing other people of being bad influences on Abbey! Practically *no*body influences Abbey, for better or for worse. She is absolutely and totally her own woman.

Anyway, I crept up and peered somewhat furtively through the glass of the lab door, and sure enough, there was Abbey perched on a stool clutching an armful of books to her bosom and looking suitably attentive, and there was Willy in her white lab coat looking a fright as usual. I remember thinking that she really was the most hideous old bag—not that she was all that old. About fifty, probably; not actually decrepit. But it does annoy one when people go around conforming to the very worst kind of stereotype; i.e., spinster science mistress equals clumpy shoes, frumpy clothes, bird's-nest hair, horn-rimmed specs and not a shred of make-up anywhere to be seen. I mean, it really isn't necessary, and what's more it's an affront.

Since she and Abbey were obviously going to be there for the duration I wandered off in search of Zoot and bumped instead into Mrs Hall (Head of English). She said, 'Ah, Robyn! Have you seen the cast list?' I grinned and said, 'Yes.'

'I'm organizing a read-through for some time next week. Any chance of David being back by then, do you think?'

'Mm . . . don't know about next week. Week after, maybe.'

'He'll be all right for the performance, I take it?'

'Gosh,' I said, 'I should think so!' The performance was weeks away—months away. Not until right at the end of term.

'I just wanted to make sure . . . we couldn't very well have a Benedick with his leg in plaster!'

'Oh, it won't be,' I said. 'Not by then.' I was looking forward to playing Beatrice to David's Benedick. I didn't want the part being taken off him and given to someone else. Specially not Pilch, who was the most obvious second choice. Not that I really had anything *against* Pilch; just that he wasn't David.

It was lunch-time before I met up with Abbey.

'So what was Willie going on about?' I said, as we messed with macaroni cheese in the canteen. (It was either macaroni cheese, chopped toad or foul flan, masquerading as sardine quiche. Experience had taught that macaroni cheese was the one least likely to poison you.)

'Oh—' Abbey waved her fork, evasively. She knew my feelings about Willie. Abbey herself, for some unfathomable, Abbey sort of reason, had always had a bit of a soft spot for the ghastly old crab. 'Basically she

44

just wanted to know if I'd like to go round and have tea with her one day after school.'

'Cor! Tea already! Get that!'

Abbey looked pained: I was behaving like David and Zoot. Somehow I just couldn't help it where Willie was concerned.

'You want to watch it,' I said. 'She's after your body.'

She wasn't, of course: she was after Abbey's mind. She wanted to make sure that she netted it for university.

'Do you have to be so ridiculous?' said Abbey.

'She's a dyke,' I said.

Abbey looked at me.

'She is. She's lezzy. Used to live with that freak that did home ec.'

'So what?' said Abbey.

'Well—' I swished with my fork in the stinking midden that was macaroni cheese. 'Like I said, you want to watch it.'

'Oh, Robyn!' Abbey spoke impatiently. 'Stop being so sexist! All she wants to do is tell me about university.'

'So are you going to go?'

'I expect I will. When David's back.'

'When he's *back*?'

'Well, I mean . . . it's difficult at the moment. Him being in hospital. His mother said I can go and visit every night if I want.'

Which of course she did; now that she had broken the ice.

'So what else did she have to say? Old Willie the Wilk?'

There was a pause. Abbey seemed uncomfortable—reluctant, almost.

'Oh! She just—'

'Just what?'

'Well—' The macaroni cheese was fast congealing into a glutinous mass. I don't think they ever actually used real cheese; I think what they used was those plastic strips. 'She was just a bit concerned about things.'

'What things?'

'Me and David.'

'You and *David*?' I was flabbergasted. The cheek of the woman!

'Oh, she didn't lecture me, or anything like that.' Abbey assured me of it, earnestly. 'I mean, she quite understood that I'd want to go and visit him. It's just that in a *general* way she sort of—well! wondered if we weren't seeing a bit too much of each other.'

'Flaming nerve! What's it got to do with her?'

'She is supposed to be our pastoral tutor.' (Mine too, worse luck.) 'She's only doing her job.'

'Her job isn't to *pry*.'

'She wasn't prying! I told you . . . she was just a bit concerned.'

'About what, for goodness' sake?'

'Oh, you know . . . people getting tied up when they're too young to know what they're doing. All that sort of stuff.'

'All that crap!'

Abbey remained silent.

'She's just scared you might suddenly take it into your head to get married and start breeding instead of going to university.'

That brought a blush to her cheek.

'There's no danger of that!'

'Well, *I* know there isn't. She obviously thinks there might be. I bet she thinks David's a bad influence.'

'No. She doesn't think that.' Abbey's tone was reproachful. 'She's not unfair.'

'Just a man-hater.'

'Robyn, she isn't! You've got her all wrong.'

So if I had, whose fault was that? If people will insist on flobbing around like sacks of cold porridge, what can they expect?

'Willie's OK,' said Abbey. 'Honestly.'

I just grunted.

Everybody kept wanting to know about David: how was he, when was he coming back? Abbey didn't know. She went to see him every single night, as his mother had said she could, but still it seemed there was nothing positive to report. Barney (Mr Barnabas, cricket, soccer and sport in general) was anxious about his precious cricket team. He kept agitating, would David be back in time for the match against Hyrst Hill? It was terribly important that he should be back in time for that! Hyrst Hill were our greatest rivals. If we could only beat Hyrst Hill, we should be in with a chance for the something-or-other challenge cup. It was absolutely *essential* that David should be there to open the batting.

'Now, tell me! What exactly are they doing to him? Is it a plaster job? I have to know! Am I going to have a fit opening bat or am I not?'

Abbey couldn't help him: she knew no more than anybody else. She grumbled to me that it was all very well, Barney raving on like an idiot, but if he hadn't insisted on David playing in his stupid football match against St Joseph's when it was perfectly obvious he shouldn't have done, then 'none of this would ever have happened . . . it's no use getting on at *me*.'

I'm afraid that I was almost as bad as Barney: *I* kept

47

getting on at her, as well.

'What about Benedick? What about the play? He'll be all right for the play, won't he?' And then, when in her exasperation she snapped, 'How should I know? I'm not a crystal ball gazer!'—'Why don't you *ask*?' I said. 'That's what I'd do.'

'How can I?' said Abbey. 'It's up to his parents.'

'Well, then, ask *them*!'

'I have.'

'So what did they say?'

'They just said they don't know.'

It was all very unsatisfactory. In the end, growing sick of me, Abbey somewhat tetchily suggested that I went along with her on Sunday afternoon and that *I* asked.

'But there won't be any doctors around on a Sunday afternoon,' I said.

'You can't ask the *doctors*,' said Abbey. She sounded horrified. (Bother the doctors? Sooner apply direct to God!) 'I meant, ask David.'

'What's the point of that? If he knew, he'd have told you!' There was a pause. 'Well?' I said. 'Wouldn't he?'

Abbey heaved a sigh.

'I suppose so,' she said; but I wasn't altogether sure that she was convinced.

I went along on Sunday, with *Much Ado* tucked under my arm, and we giggled quite a lot about various things—about Willie being after Abbey's body, and Big Jane Dorning dropping one of her famous clangers (she had translated *l'enceinte royale*, which of course means the royal enclosure, as the royal pregnancy)—but somehow I didn't feel that the visit was a success. I don't know whether it was the presence of parents (always a bit inhibiting) or the fact that Zoot wasn't there, but the merriment and jollity seemed forced, as if it were all a bit of an effort; and furthermore nobody but me seemed to have any real *interest* in anything. David flipped through the pages of *Much Ado* and we glanced at a few key scenes together, but I could tell his heart wasn't in it. He was only doing it out of politeness, to keep me happy.

I said, 'Mrs Hall keeps nagging at me to know when you're going to be back, and poor old Barney's doing his bits and pieces over some match or other. What was it?' I looked across at Abbey. 'Hyrst Hill?' Abbey nodded, and said yes. 'He's desperate to know whether he's going to have an opening bat.'

I waited for David to say something, but even before he could open his mouth his mother had gone and stepped in.

'Hyrst Hill—that's the independent school, isn't it? The one with the stripy uniform?'

Abbey nodded again and said, 'Yes, that's right'; and lo and behold! before I knew it we had launched into a full rundown of every school within a fifty-mile radius. We'd just about reached bottom-of-the-barrel stage—'What's that one with the funny name?' 'What's that one with the blue and gold?'—when the bell clanged for the end of visiting and I hadn't managed to find out a single thing.

I accepted a lift home from David's parents (they talked about *schools* the entire way) and arrived back just in time for tea. I spent the rest of the evening learning my lines from Act I.

4

It must have been the week following that visit to David—that visit when we all talked so earnestly and at such length about things that didn't matter—that I woke one morning to a terrible feeling of gloom and despair. It may simply have been the fact that it was raining, or that I had a spot coming to fruition on my chin, or even that the Windbag had been threatening us with another of his moralizing lunch-time lectures. I don't know; I can't now remember. I can't even remember which day of the week it was, though I tend to believe it must have been either a Wednesday or a Thursday. But I'm not really sure. All I'm really sure of is that my gloom and despair turned out to be what I think are known as self-fulfilling prophecies: it was a ghastly, horrible day.

I'd arrived at school and was trundling across the playground going over some of my Beatrice lines in readiness for the rehearsal that evening, hoping that David would be back soon so that I could act opposite him instead of opposite Pilch, who, as predicted, had been picked to stand in for him, when I became aware of a small figure jigging somewhat anxiously at my side. I looked down and saw that it was Sophie. I said, 'Hi, Soph! What are you doing?'

In reply to which, instead of saying, 'Jigging up and down' or 'Going into school' she said, 'Abbey's not coming in today.'

'Really?' I said. 'Why's that?'

Sophie fiddled with the catch of her briefcase.

'Says she's got a headache.'

That surprised me. Abbey almost never had head-aches—and certainly never stayed away from school. Also, the way Sophie put it, *says she's got a headache*, made it sound as if it were just an excuse.

'You mean, she hasn't really?' I said.

Sophie hunched her shoulders. She was still fid-dling with the catch on her briefcase, snapping it backwards and forwards.

'You'll break that,' I said, 'if you keep playing with it.'

Still she went on doing it. It was like some kind of nervous affliction.

'Did she ask you to tell me?' I said.

Sophie shook her head. She is very much like Abbey to look at, except that her face is a bit rounder, her eyes wide open and full of what can only be called perpetual wonderment. Sophie, even now, has an air of child-like innocence about her. Abbey never had that. She has always been serious and committed beyond her years.

We walked on together, Sophie and I, Sophie flick-ing at her catch, me, with one part of my mind wondering about Abbey, with the other trying to get back into my lines.

I thank God and my cold blood, I am of your humour for that. I had rather hear my dog bark at a—

'Robyn?' said Sophie.

'Mm?'

Flick flick flick, went the catch on her briefcase.

'Is David going to die?'

Just for a moment, the world stood still. All the figures in the playground stopped moving, and at the same time became very little and distant, whilst all about me the hubbub of their voices receded, blurred to muted echoes dimly heard.

Sophie touched timidly at my hand.

'Robyn?' she said.

The figures started moving again: babel returned.

'Sophie, honestly!' I said. 'What a thing to say! Of *course* he isn't!'

Her cheeks had turned bright pink. You could tell, looking at her, that she was hideously embarrassed (not wishing to make a fool of herself) yet determined nonetheless to stick to her guns. I admired her for it, though it did rather alarm me. What could have given her such a macabre idea?

'Has someone said something to you?'

'Abbey spoke to his parents.' She was back to her fiddling again, not wanting to look at me. 'He's got to have an operation.'

'Oh! Is *that* all!' I laughed—and Sophie blushed scarlet to the roots of her hair. I knew I'd been unkind, but just for a minute she'd really rattled me. 'An operation isn't anything.' (Oh, vainglorious Robyn! She who screamed the place down when merely being given a humble anti-tetanus jab . . .) 'Loads of people have operations —Zoot had one when he broke his collar bone. *You* had one when you had your appendix out. You didn't die, did you?'

'No,' said Sophie. Her lip trembled. 'But Abbey's locked herself in her room and she's crying.'

Abbey? Abbey crying? That rattled me all over again: that rattled me even worse. Abbey doesn't cry; she just isn't a crying sort of person. I wanted to ask Sophie more, but the bell had gone for assembly and I couldn't. In assembly I looked for Zoot, but he wasn't there. I remember him not being there, though I can't now remember why he wasn't (practising in the beloved nets, most likely). Another thing I can't remember is actually sitting through the morning's classes, waiting for the moment when I could get away and ring Abbey. It was lunch-time before I did so. (I wonder, looking back on it, why I didn't do it immediately? It seems inconceivable, now, that I *could* have sat through the morning's classes. But I did.)

Zoot wasn't around when I slipped out of school and went down to the call-box at the end of the road. Maybe at that stage I still hadn't spoken with him. (Maybe at that stage I still wasn't really convinced that Sophie wasn't just a lovelorn second-year indulging in a bit of melodrama.) It was Abbey's mother who answered the telephone.

'Hallo, Mrs Johnson!' I said. 'It's Robyn here.'

'Oh! Robyn—' She sounded sort of relieved and yet anxious at the same time. But Abbey's mother is quite an anxious sort of person.

'I was wondering,' I said, 'how Abbey was.'

'She's all right.' Now she sounded guarded; cautious. Not sure how much she ought to give away. 'Just a bit peaky.'

Peaky! What an odd word.

'Sophie said she had a headache.'

'Yes. Well—that is—' Pause. 'Perhaps you'd better have a word with her.'

It was several seconds before Abbey came to the telephone.

'Robyn?' she said. Her voice sounded all clogged and constricted; it was the voice of someone who didn't quite trust herself to speak. 'Where are you calling from?'

'Coin box.'

'School?'

'No, outside. What's going on? Sophie said—'

'What did Sophie say?' She came in very sharply on that. I hesitated.

53

'She said you . . . had a headache.' I couldn't very well tell her that Sophie had said she was up in her bedroom crying—especially as I suspected that she still was. Crying, I mean. I'd never known Abbey cry before. Come to that, I don't think she'd ever known me. It's not the sort of thing you do in front of people. Well, you do when you're in infants, of course; when you're in infants you cry all over the place in front of absolutely anyone without thinking twice about it. (That's one of the joys of being in infants.) As you get older you grow more secretive, so that crying becomes something you only do in the privacy of your own room late at night with the lights turned out. It upset me, sensing that at the other end of the telephone Abbey was standing weeping. My eyes got all hot and itchy without even knowing what it was that she was weeping for.

'Abbey?' I said. 'You OK?'

She obviously wasn't; she didn't even attempt to say that she was. I mean normally you cover things up, you grunt if you can't manage actual speech, you go 'Mm!' as brightly as ever you can and then the other person gets happy because that lets them off the hook and they can just babble inanities until you've pulled yourself together. I couldn't do that with Abbey. Not that I can't babble inanities with the best of them, in fact it's one of my most prized social assets, but when your best friend is silently sobbing her heart out at the other end of a telephone line you can't pretend not to notice.

'Shall I come round?' I said.

'Yes.' Abbey drew a breath; deep and tremulous. 'Come round.'

'We've got a rehearsal after school, I'll come as soon as it's over—or would you rather I came before?'

Abbey said no, come when the rehearsal was finished; they would wait tea for me. I said OK, I'd get there as soon as I could. I then rang off and called home, to let Mumps know what was happening.

'We've got a rehearsal,' I said, 'and then I'm going round to Abbey's. I don't know what time I'll be back, it might not be until late. Is that OK?'

Generally, parents being what they are, Mumps would have started wittering about tomorrow being a school day and to make sure I didn't miss the last bus, and *whatever I did* not to accept a lift from anyone. Today she said, 'That's all right, stay as long as you like. Stay the night if you want. Just so long as you let us know.' I didn't think anything of it at the time.

Just as I don't really remember the first half of that day, neither do I very clearly remember the second. I suppose I talked to Zoot—I *must* have talked to Zoot —but I have no actual recollection of doing so. I do remember attending the rehearsal after school, because I remember Mrs Hall asking me if there was any news of David yet, and I said, 'I think they're going to have to operate.'

'Oh, dear!' she said. 'Does that mean plaster?'

I said I supposed that it did, but that it was bound to be off long before the end of term.

'Yes,' said Pilch, 'but you have to learn to walk again. I had a cousin broke his leg, he couldn't walk properly on it for months.'

I thought that was pretty mean of Pilch—just trying to snitch the lead part for himself.

'I don't see that it would matter,' I said, 'if Benedick walked with a limp. After all, he's a soldier, he could have got wounded.'

'Oh, yes?'

'Yes,' I said. I wasn't having Pilch at *any* price; not now. 'Why shouldn't he?'

'Why should he?' said Pilch.

I could have hit him.

Imagine . . . I actually stayed for the whole of that rehearsal: from four o'clock till half past five. How could I? *Knowing* that Abbey was in distress and that she wanted me? Why didn't I tell Mrs Hall and cut the wretched thing? Mrs Hall wouldn't have minded. She was one of the nice ones; not sour and man-hating like Willie, or eaten up with senile jealousy like the Windbag. She would have understood.

It must have been about ten minutes to six when I arrived at Glenthorne Avenue, where the Johnsons live. (The house is called Dunroamin, it actually *is*. But it's not the Johnsons' fault, it was called that when they bought it.) Abbey herself opened the door to me. I was relieved to see that she wasn't crying still, though her eyes were all swollen and terribly red —what Zoot would have called pissoles in the snow.

We didn't waste time on preliminaries. There wasn't any 'Robyn! You've come!' or 'Abbey, what's wrong?' Abbey just said, 'I've got tea upstairs,' and we went up together to her room, where so often in the past we'd sat and giggled and tried on clothes and discussed nice cosy things such as whether or not to shave our armpits and what we thought it would be like to have sex. It was there, pouring tea out of an old earthenware teapot, so that she could concentrate on the tea cups and not have to meet my gaze, that Abbey told me: David had a tumour and they were going to have to amputate . . .

I remember, after she'd told me, I just sat there stunned. I think I probably said something pathetic like, 'Oh, Abbey, no!' or 'Oh, my God!' Like something out of a bad script. I remember Abbey being determinedly calm and matter-of-fact (she said afterwards that she had decided that my arrival was to be her deadline for tears: from that point on she was going to face up to things and be positive). She told me that David had known what was wrong with him for almost a week but hadn't been able to bring himself to break the news to her; that finally he had asked his parents to do it for him, and last night they had done so.

'I couldn't have rung you,' she said. 'I just couldn't have talked.'

She didn't have to explain: *my* immediate thought was, how to tell Zoot? I could no more have rung him, that night, than Abbey could have rung me the night before.

'But we can't *not* tell him.' Abbey, I remember, was terribly anxious on this point—almost as if she were seizing on it for the focus of all her worries. 'It wouldn't be right if we knew and not Zoot.'

I agreed that it wouldn't. After all, Zoot had been David's best mate since almost the very beginning. I promised that I would be the one to tell him.

'Tomorrow?' said Abbey. 'Before school?'

I could see that she wanted to avoid any possibility of Zoot bumping into her before he bumped into me. I could see that it would be agony for her if he were to go bouncing up in his usual Zoot-like fashion, slap-on-the-back, gung-ho-on-the-Rialto kind of thing—yes, and what of the Windbag and his walking wounded? Any more cracks like that, once Zoot knew how things stood, and I wouldn't answer for the consequences. But who was going to tell *him*? Who was going to tell Barney? Who was going to tell Mrs Hall? *I wonder you will still be talking, Signior Benedick . . .*

'Oh, Abbey!' I said.

'Don't! Please, Robyn . . . don't!' I remember Abbey pursing her lips, very tight, until the moment had passed; then smiling at me, all sort of bright and brave and defiant, thrusting her hair back over her shoulders. 'Don't go and set me off again. I've been through all that. I'm all right now. I've got to grips with it. The thing to do'—she took a breath—'the thing to do is to be positive.'

'You're right,' I said; and I sat up very straight on the edge of the bed and nodded, emphatically, to show that she had my support.

'Being negative is the very worst thing.'

'Yes, it is,' I said.

'All the books say that it's your *attitude* that matters.'

'Yes, because it can rub off. If you're negative, then it can make the other person negative as well.'

'Whereas if one is *positive*—'

Positive! It was a word that we clung to. Being positive meant putting up barriers in one's brain —barriers to keep out the really *bad* thoughts and only let through the ones that were bearable. The ones that could be coped with, such as when were they going to operate (on Friday, Abbey said) and how long would it be before David could come back to school? One could cope with the thought of an operation: operations cured things. One could even (just about) cope with the thought of a David coming back who couldn't play football or cricket. What one couldn't cope with was the thought of David never coming back at all, and so one didn't think about that. To think about it would be negative; and being negative could rub off.

We talked, while we ate sandwiches and fruit

cake—Abbey apologized for being able to eat, she seemed to think that it showed lack of sensitivity, but I said it was only sensible because there wasn't any point in her making herself ill, was there? *That* wouldn't help David. She confessed, then, that it was the first food that had passed her lips all day—we talked of all the most positive things, Abbey and I, that we could think of. I said, 'Do you remember that girl—what's her name? I can't remember her name . . . that girl that had her leg off and then went mountain climbing?' and Abbey said, 'Oh, yes, I *know*. There are hundreds of cases.'

'I mean, probably,' I said, 'with modern surgery and everything—'

'Oh, they can do all sorts of things,' said Abbey.

'It's not like it would have been, say, when our parents were young.'

'Heavens, no! It must have been terrible, then.'

'And Clearhaven *is* a good hospital.'

'And there is your father,' said Abbey; meaning, I suppose, that at least we had a channel of communication. It wasn't as if David had fallen into the hands of total strangers.

I thought about Pop. Did *he* know, I wondered? And then I realized that of course he must do. He must have known almost as long as David; the hospital would have been in touch. And if Pop knew, then Mumps would also know, because he always told her things. I suddenly saw it all —why it was they hadn't wanted to talk about David when I had asked them last week; why Mumps, when I had telephoned her at lunch-time, had said, 'Stay the night if you want.' I had a moment of indignation—that they should have known and should have kept it from me! But then, if they had told me . . . how would I ever have found the courage to break it to Abbey? David hadn't been able to, and I didn't know that I would have, either.

At half past six Abbey suddenly sprang up and said that she must get ready, she had to leave for the hospital in twenty minutes. (I immediately felt bad at having arrived so late and wished that I'd cut the rehearsal.) She said that that morning she hadn't thought she would be able to face going in and seeing David, but now she had got herself more together she knew that *not* to go would be a betrayal; and because I felt so mean about having stayed on at the rehearsal I asked if she'd like me to go with her, but she said no, she thought she would be able to cope with it better if she were by herself. I was secretly rather relieved about that. I'm quite good in most social situations —well, you have to be if you want to get on in the theatre—but this was one I'd never come up against. I mean, I'd been to visit my grandmother when she'd had a stroke, but it's different having a stroke when you're seventy-six and having what David had when you're only seventeen. I thought it showed immense courage on Abbey's part, though when I told her so she said, 'David's the one that needs courage, not me.' Actually, I thought they both did.

Abbey was naturally anxious about what she should wear. I could guess what she was thinking: she didn't want to turn up looking all dim and depressing (because of being positive) but on the other hand it was hardly the right occasion for tarting oneself up like a Christmas tree. I said, 'Something cheerful but in good taste,' which wasn't really much help because Abbey's clothes always are in good taste, I'm the one that goes in for all the screaming pinks and puke greens. In the end she chose a blue pleated skirt, blue waistcoat, white blouse and sandals. All very neat and demure and the sort of gear I wouldn't have been seen dead in, but it suited Abbey. With her hair loose about her shoulders she managed to look sexy as well as demure (though I don't think she quite realized this: if she had she probably wouldn't have done it, and that would have been a pity because in my experience the masculine morale, however low, is always perked up by thoughts of *the other*).

'I don't look as if I've been howling,' she said, 'do I?'

'Well . . . you are a tidge rheumy.'

Abbey almost never uses make-up, so it was a bit of a job trying to repair the damage without making her look different from how she usually looks—which, as I pointed out, would be the last thing David wanted; but I managed to fix her up, with a touch of this and that, and the old theatrical sleight of hand, and we set off on tiptoe down the stairs. The reason we were on tiptoe was that Abbey had this idea of getting out of the house without anyone accosting us. I said, 'Oughtn't I to stop and say hallo to your mother?' but Abbey said no, just *come*.

I suppose what it was, she wasn't feeling up to the demands of her family. Mr and Mrs Johnson are dear, *sweet* people, but Mrs Johnson really is the most terrible worrier. Also, they both happened to be extremely fond of David. The son they had never had, and so forth. They always said that he was a good lad (of course, *they* had never heard the celebrated double act) so that now, being the sort of family they were, i.e. supportive, united, hold-together-in-times-of-trouble, they were probably only too eager to pour forth upon Abbey their comfort and understanding. I could quite see that just at this moment it was something she felt she couldn't handle.

61

As it happened, it was Sophie rather than Mrs Johnson who caught us. She was lying in wait at the foot of the stairs. She didn't say anything as we approached, nor even as we reached the ground floor; just silently stood aside to let us pass. But then, as Abbey opened the front door: 'Are you going to see David?' she said.

'Yes,' said Abbey. She said it rather curtly. I knew that she didn't mean to be curt; it was just her way of protecting herself.

'Do you want to send him a message?' I said. I felt sorry for Sophie, standing there all forlorn in the middle of the hall. I could sense that she was feeling excluded. Something was wrong, she'd picked up that much, but nobody was telling her what it was. When I asked if she wanted to send a message she nodded, shyly, but at the same time cast a wary eye in Abbey's direction. 'Abbey will give him your love,' I said, 'won't you?'

'Yes,' said Abbey. She jerked her head. 'Come *on*!'

I went with her on the bus; it seemed the least I could do. (It took me loads of stops out of my way, so it was a sort of tiny sacrifice. *Very* tiny.) We didn't talk much on the journey. I couldn't think of anything to say except, 'Give David my love.' Probably everyone had sent him their love—me, Sophie, Abbey's parents.

'His sister's coming over,' said Abbey. She said it apropos (if that's the right expression) of nothing in particular—I mean, just suddenly, sitting there on the bus, looking out of the window . . . 'His sister's coming over.'

I said, 'The one in Malawi?' which was a silly thing to say, because I knew very well that David only had the one sister. He also had a brother, Edward, whom

62

everyone called Ned. Ned lived at home but worked in London, as an auctioneer. Judith was a teacher who was married to a biologist who did things on a plantation. They were both quite a lot older than David. Abbey and I knew Ned just a little, but we'd never met Judith. The last time she'd visited England had been way back in our second year, before we were a foursome.

'He told me the other day,' said Abbey; and I noticed her fingers lacing themselves together as she spoke. 'She's coming now because she's expecting a baby in August and they don't let you fly when you're more than eight months pregnant.'

'I suppose they're scared of things happening in mid-flight,' I said. It was only later, after we'd parted company, that I realized the significance of what she was trying to tell me. At the time I thought she was just making conversation.

We reached the hospital, and I walked with her to the gates.

'Are you sure you don't want me to come in with you?' I said.

Abbey shook her head. 'Honestly . . . I'll be OK.'

'I'll see you tomorrow, then—'

'And you will tell Zoot?'

'Yes,' I said. 'I'll tell him.'

I left Abbey (I didn't glance over my shoulder and look back at her: I suppose I'm quite superstitious, really), crossed the square and turned up towards the High Street and my own bus stop. And it was there, waiting for a number five to take me back to Park-mead, that it suddenly hit me: when Abbey had said that David's sister was coming over, what she meant was that she was coming over *to see David*. She was coming all the way from Malawi just to see him. And she was coming now because she was expecting a baby in August and they won't let you fly when you're more than eight months pregnant . . .

Sophie's little voice from this morning, pathetic and frightened, sounded in my ears: 'Robyn . . . is David going to die?'

Die? *Die?* A wave of panic swept over me. People our age didn't die!

Yes, they did. They died from all sorts of things. They fell into rivers and drowned, they ran into roads and got run over, sometimes they even got murdered. But that was different! That was accidents—things that could be avoided. They didn't die from *illness*.

They did. They died all the time from illness. They died from leukaemia. They died from kidney disease. They died from tumours . . .

But not David! Not David! Please, God, not David! David was so beautiful—so golden. People like David didn't die! It was people like Avril Ellison—pale, weedy, hunch-shouldered people. People with pigeon toes and knock knees and the sniffles. *They* were the people that died. Not people like David!

My thoughts on the way home were all negative. I tried to keep the barriers up, because I *do* believe in the power of positive thinking, but it wasn't any use, negativity just kept seeping through until finally it overwhelmed me. By the time I left the bus at Park-mead my heart was pounding in its cage, my head splitting open with the horror of it all. I remember thinking, this is like a nightmare . . . it's like a night-mare! I suppose in moments of deepest stress one tends to think in clichés. I suppose they would never have become clichés in the first place if they didn't represent the common experience.

My parents were watching television when I got in.

Mumps took one look at me and said, 'I'll get you a cup of tea.'

'Brandy,' said Pop. 'A good stiff brandy.'

Mumps looked doubtful. 'Do you really think she ought?'

Pop said, 'Yes, I do—and I'll have one while you're about it.'

I noticed that he'd turned the television off. It takes a lot for him to do that—he always says it makes excellent wallpaper at the end of a hard day's work.

Mumps handed me a brandy bubble. (I *loathe* brandy; but that night I drank the lot without even realizing.) 'How is Abbey?' she said.

'She's gone to see David.'

There was a pause.

'Did she—tell you?'

'Yes.' I looked across at Pop. 'It's serious,' I said, 'isn't it?'

Silently, Pop inclined his head.

I remember taking a swig of brandy. I remember it, because it very nearly choked me. The back of my throat was practically flayed raw.

'Is he—' I tried to say, 'Is he going to die?' but I couldn't. I just couldn't get the words out. I'm obviously not as brave as Sophie was. 'I know you can't discuss patients,' I said, 'but—once they've operated—I mean—that'll be it, won't it?'

They looked at me, gravely.

'I mean, he's not going to *die*,' I said, 'is he? Not with treatment, and everything? I mean . . . not these days . . . '

My voice trailed off. Pop said: 'Modern medicine does have an extremely powerful armoury of drugs at its disposal.'

It wasn't the answer that I had wanted. I had

wanted him to say, 'Die? Good God in heaven, no! A patient of mine?' But Pop has never been one to beat about bushes. He has always believed in a policy of being brutally frank, on the grounds that any other course leads to mistrust and suspicion. Mumps is the one who goes in for pill-sweetening. I'd always thought, until now, that I preferred Pop's way. If he'd said that David wasn't going to die, then I'd have known that I could believe him; whereas if Mumps had said it—but neither of them had. Pop had as good as spelt it out for me: David *could* die. It didn't mean that he was going to, but he *could*. Because people did. For once I thought that I would rather have had the pill sweetened just a little bit.

Mumps did try. David was young, she said, and strong; he wouldn't give up without a fight. And look at that girl—that athlete—what was her name? That one that had had exactly the same problem as David: *she* was climbing mountains. Mumps brought it out with such an air of triumph—just as I had, for Abbey.

Oh, that girl, whoever she was! Nobody ever *could* remember her name, but she was our talisman, our magical white rabbit which every now and again, to renew our vows of positivity, we would produce, with a flourish, from the hat. I think you need a symbol of some kind, and she was ours. Even Pop could not deny that she was climbing mountains . . .

We sat there all evening, Mumps and Pop and me, talking things over. They were very good; they treated me like an adult, as someone who was responsible and to be trusted. I was grateful to them for that. I felt that if I were to be of any support to Abbey then there were things I needed to know.

What I didn't understand, I said, was how just a little unimportant incident like Sable crushing David's leg against a tree could make *this* happen, but Pop explained how it wasn't Sable who had made it happen, Sable had only produced the symptoms of something that was already there. That, to me, seemed really creepy. To think that *things* can be there—that this particular *thing* could have been there for ages—and nobody knowing, but when I told Pop he simply shook his head and said, 'I'm afraid it's in the nature of the beast.'

He explained to me a little bit about the operation that David was to have on Friday and what it would involve, and I forced myself to listen even though the very thought of anaesthetics and being cut open is enough, as a rule, to make me turn green. (I haven't actually got a very strong stomach.) Mumps told me about attitude being important and how we must all (meaning Zoot and Abbey and me) strive to be positive, and especially when we went to see David because 'he'll need all the help he can get.' I said that Abbey and I had already decided upon that, and Mumps said that Abbey was a good, sensible girl and 'worth her weight in gold'.

'But it's not going to be easy for her, you know. You'll have to be prepared to make allowances.'

I thought that it wasn't going to be very easy for David, either; but it wasn't until I was in bed that night that it occurred to me . . . we had all been discussing things from *our* point of view—how *we* should approach the problem, how *we* were feeling about it—but nobody, as yet, had actually sat down and imagined how it must be to be David.

I knew why when I tried: it was just too awful.

5

I kept my word to Abbey. I rang Zoot before breakfast the next morning and said there was something I had to tell him and that it was urgent. I had to see him, I said, before school.

I wonder if Zoot had any premonition what it was about? I think he must have done, for he didn't make any of his usual jokey comments, or groan at the prospect of having to bestir himself and leave home fifteen minutes earlier than usual. He didn't even ask any questions. He just said, 'OK. Where?' We arranged to meet in the gardens in the centre of town, near where I got off the bus.

Zoot was there waiting for me when I arrived.

'Is it David?' he said.

I nodded.

'Is it something bad?'

I had to take a breath before I could speak.

'Let's go into the gardens,' I said.

It was there, in the gardens, by a municipal flower bed displaying the message WELCOME TO CLEARHAVEN in mixed rows of begonias and lobelia, that I told him. Zoot said, 'Oh, Jesus!' And then, 'Oh, Jesus, oh, God! That piss awful joke!'

I said, 'What piss awful joke?'

'That joke,' he said; and his voice sounded all cracked and honking like it did when it was going through its breaking phase. 'That piss awful bloody joke . . . taking his leg off . . . '

'It wasn't your fault! You weren't to know.'

'You don't think D— '

'No! Nobody did.'

'But they must have wondered,' said Zoot, 'or they wouldn't have rushed him in.'

I remembered, when Zoot said that, remarking to Abbey that 'that was quick' and Abbey somewhat impatiently telling me that you couldn't let people go walking about with broken bones, could you? I remembered the morning I saw David at the surgery, and his mother being there with him; the way she could only just about bring herself to smile at me, and hadn't said hallo or anything. *Had* they wondered, all those weeks ago? (It seemed like all those weeks ago: in fact, it was only two.)

'*They* might have suspected,' I said; all the medical people, the people like Pop. 'But they wouldn't have said anything to David.'

To his mother, maybe; but not to David. It was very important to me to believe that they hadn't said anything to David. I couldn't bear the thought that we might have sat there in the hospital, on that first visit, exchanging tasteless badinage about female flesh and him pretending to laugh and be amused while all the time dreading that they might find what they had said they might. Bad enough remembering the *second* visit, when I knew now what David had known then: that was crucifixion enough. I suppose poor old Zoot felt the same about his awful bloody joke.

'There's no point in torturing yourself,' I said. I said it as much for my own sake as for Zoot's. 'What we have to do now is be positive.'

We walked on, around the flower beds, being as positive as we could. I told Zoot about the girl who climbed mountains and Zoot speculated as to David being able to swim and carry on riding.

'Well, if people can go *climbing*,' I said; and I told him

69

what Pop had told me about how they would fit a temporary prosthesis (it sounded better than artificial leg, and anyway it wasn't really, that would come later) a week or so after the operation, which meant that by the end of the first month he would actually be able to start walking again. 'I mean, that's pretty good,' I said, 'isn't it? After just a month?'

Zoot agreed that it was; and we both agreed that if he kept up that sort of progress he'd practically be back to normal by the end of term.

'By this time *next* year he'll probably even be able to play cricket.'

We settled for cricket rather than football. Football, we thought, would be a bit too much of a rough house; but *cricket* . . . everybody knew that cricket was a gentleman's game.

We had just solemnly congratulated each other on the fact of David being a batsman rather than a bowler when Zoot suddenly looked stricken again.

'What do I tell Barney?' he said.

Not only Barney but Mrs Hall, and the Wind-bag—everybody else, for the matter of that. It was the same thought as had occurred to me.

'We'd better ask Abbey,' I said.

We were a bit hesitant, the pair of us, about going up to Abbey that first morning. Zoot was wanting to communicate sympathy and understanding, without quite knowing how to set about it (sympathy and understanding not being much in Zoot's line: he is more of a jolly ho-ho sort of person) whereas I, remembering the distress Abbey had been in yesterday, was simply terrified of saying anything which might set her crying.

I needn't have worried: Abbey is a very controlled sort of person. Once she has come to a decision—in

70

this case, that there were to be no more tears—she always stands by it. She was waiting for us at the school gates. Zoot said, 'Robyn told me,' and Abbey just nodded, quite calm, and said, 'Yes.' And the way that she said it made it clear she knew exactly how Zoot was feeling. He didn't have to do anything special by way of communicating.

I asked her how David was. Abbey hesitated; then, 'He's all right,' she said. We left it at that. (She never did give me any details of that visit when they both of them knew that the other had been told: I have never pressed her.)

Zoot wanted to know what we did about Barney, and Mrs Hall, and the Windbag. Abbey said that David's mother had spoken to her about that last night. They—David's parents—were going to come in that morning and talk to Mr Francis, the Head Master (who is now retired—Willie, of all people, has taken his place) and they were going to ask that an announcement be made, if not to the whole school then at least to our year.

'Is that what David wants?' I said.

Abbey said yes, it was David who had suggested it. His mother had agreed, but had decided, with Abbey, that the announcement should be held over until Monday, by which time he would have had the operation.

'Just so long as that arseole doesn't make any more of his smart remarks,' said Zoot.

He meant, of course, the Great Rhetorical. But I think, somehow, word must have filtered through, because there weren't any smart remarks any more; not then or ever again. Not even someone as twisted as the Windbag could be jealous now.

I can't remember whether it was the Wednesday or

the Thursday that I broke the news to Zoot. The next clear memory I have is of Friday—the day when David was to be operated on. For some reason the operation wasn't scheduled to take place until late in the afternoon. I always think of these things as happening in the morning, I don't know why; perhaps because the morning gives less time for chewing at fingernails and imagining ghastly things going wrong. (It can't just be me who imagines ghastly things going wrong. Pop always says that *any* operation which proceeds under a general anaesthetic contains an element of risk, but he also points out that that element is practically negligible compared with some that we take for granted, like driving around in cars, for example. I'm sure he's right, for Pop is not the person to make such claims lightly; and anyway, as I kept reminding myself, we hadn't sat around and chewed our fingers to the bone when Zoot had had his operation. *Operations.* Zoot had had so many. But Zoot's had all been minor. As I kept trying *not* to remind myself, what they had done to Zoot had been as nothing to what they were going to do to David . . .)

It was a bad day, that Friday. What made it worse, in some ways, was that we were the only ones who knew. Abbey said it would have been worse if we *hadn't* been the only ones to know. She said if the others had been told she simply wouldn't have come in to school, she couldn't have faced it. I suppose that basically I am more gregarious than Abbey, or maybe I simply have more of the group mentality: I would have found comfort in the knowledge that we were all sharing the same emotions. Abbey, scornfully, said that they wouldn't be the same emotions. Ours were real, because David was our friend: theirs would only be simulated. A mass slush-in, was what she called it. I thought she was being unfair, but I forgave her because I knew what she must be going through.

It was very difficult concentrating that day. Zoot was lucky because he only had classes in the morning, the whole of the afternoon was devoted to cricket —there was a match which went on right through from two o'clock till six. (That was when I noticed the Windbag wasn't making his smart remarks any more. Normally he'd have said something sneering on the lines of 'England without W.G. Grace' and 'an oyster without any pearl'. That Friday he didn't say anything at all.)

At quarter to four Abbey went home to sit by the telephone, though she knew there couldn't possibly be any news for at least another hour. I stopped off to check the progress of the cricket match. They all looked grim and pointed at the scoreboard, and somebody asked, in tones of exasperation, when that wanker was going to be back? I was thankful that Abbey hadn't come with me. I left a message for Zoot, who was batting—or swotting flies, which was the way David always used to describe Zoot's batting technique—then went off to catch my bus and sit, like Abbey, by the telephone.

Abbey rang me just after half past five. She said that David's mother had just rung her, that the operation was over, everything had gone according to plan and that David was back on the ward. Oh, the relief! Rationalize as one may that earthquakes do *not* commonly occur in the middle of operations (especially ones taking place on the south coast of England), that mad anaesthetists with bogus degrees are *not* everyday phenomena, that supplies of oxygen do *not* normally fail and leave people to exist as vegetables, nevertheless one always does have these little niggling anxieties.

'So when are you going to see him?' I said.

Abbey said on Sunday. She said tomorrow was 'just family', which I couldn't help feeling was a bit mean, considering what David meant to her, and what she meant to David. I would have thought, if they'd been thinking of David rather than themselves, they would have said that no matter who else went to see him, Abbey must. Abbey didn't appear to feel slighted, however. She said that David's sister was going to be there, and that naturally she had to be given priority, having come all the way from Malawi, and in any case she herself was 'doing something' tomorrow. She didn't say what it was. She just said that she would give me a call on Sunday, after she had been to the hospital. In the meantime, she said, could she leave me to pass on the news to Zoot? I said that she could, yelled to Mumps, who was in the garden, that 'David's had the operation, he's OK, I'm going in to tell Zoot,' grabbed my jacket and went haring off up the road towards the bus.

The match had finished by the time I reached school. As I was going in I bumped into a boy from our year called Whingeing Osborne. Whinge was on his way out.

'We lost,' he said, as I shot past him. (Needless to say, *he* hadn't been playing: Whinge is essentially one of life's onlookers.) 'By *six wickets*.'

I flapped a hand in acknowledgement of the tragedy.

'That's because David wasn't there.' He made it sound as if it were my fault—*our* fault—Abbey's and Zoot's and mine. As if we were purposely preventing David from being there. 'Anyway,' he yelled fractiously, 'what's happening to him?'

74

I pretended not to hear. Whinge would know soon enough. All I wanted to do now was find Zoot and tell him the good news.

By way of celebration—sort of celebration—Zoot and I went into town to eat pizzas at Larry's. We always used to go to Larry's when we had anything to celebrate; and whichever way one looked at it, things *were* better now than they had been that morning. Of course we were both very well aware that an operation wasn't necessarily a cure, we weren't stupid, we weren't ostriches hiding our heads in the sand, but it did seem that it was the biggest and most dramatic of the hurdles David would have to face.

Zoot said that his dad, who worked on the railways, had told him that he knew a bloke that had fallen in front of a train and lost a leg as a result, and 'it's fantastic what he can do . . . plays golf, rides his bike, goes swimming . . . everything practically.' Zoot said that his dad had said that if you didn't know, you probably wouldn't even notice. And then, being a bit cautious, because losing a leg from having it run over by a train wasn't quite the same as losing a leg for the reason David was, 'I guess they'll have to give him some kind of treatment . . . X-rays, or something.'

'Radiotherapy,' I said. Pop had told me about it.

'Yeah . . . I guess they have to do that. Just to make sure.'

'And drugs,' I said. Pop had told me about the drugs, too. I didn't like the sound of them. 'If ever I got it,' I said, 'I wouldn't have drugs.'

Zoot stared at me—no, he didn't stare, he *glared*.

'What are you talking about, wouldn't have them?'

'I wouldn't let them give them to me.'

'Why not?' His tone was aggressive.

'They're horrible. They make your hair fall out.'

'So it grows again!'

'Yes, but not for ages.'

There was an astounded silence.

'Are you *mad*?' said Zoot.

I didn't know. Was I? I must be! Not taking life-saving drugs only because they made your hair fall out?

'That is just so *pathetic*,' said Zoot.

I hung my head. I wanted to say, 'But David wouldn't be David!' only I was too ashamed. I couldn't mean it—I couldn't be so frivolous! To place *looks* above *life*?

Zoot was still glowering at me. I felt as if I, personally, were denying David his only chance to health and happiness.

'I'll tell you *some*thing,' said Zoot. 'If you were in that position you'd grab whatever was on offer!'

'Yes,' I said, humbly. 'I expect you're right.'

'You'd better believe it,' said Zoot.

He went back, rather moodily, to his pizza. I prodded at mine with my fork. Somehow, it didn't seem much like a celebration any more. What, after all, were we celebrating? David having a leg amputated? Faced with the prospect of radiotherapy and drugs that made you feel ghastly and your hair drop out? Tremblingly, I speared a piece of pizza. It seemed a funny kind of thing to celebrate.

'Hey!' Zoot reached across and tapped me on the back of the hand. 'What's the matter?'

Suddenly, I was sobbing.

'It's so awful! It's just all s-so awful! It's—'

'Robyn!' said Zoot. 'Stop it!'

The tears flooded over me, pouring in great waterfalls down my cheeks, sploshing and splattering into my pizza.

76

'I c-can't, I c—'

'Yes, you can,' said Zoot. He rapped on the table. 'Be positive!'

'I c—'

'For David's sake!'

For David's sake—

I gulped.

'That's better,' said Zoot.

There was a silence, broken only by the chinking of distant cutlery and the occasional shuddering gasp which was me drawing breath.

The shuddering stopped. I took out my handkerchief and blew my nose, tucked my hair behind my ears, pushed my plate away from me. Be positive.

'We ought to get him something. Something that'll cheer him up. We ought to come into town tomorrow morning and get it. Then we could take it round and leave it at Abbey's. What shall we get? We could get—'

'I don't know that I can, tomorrow morning,' said Zoot. 'We've got nets until—' He stopped. 'Sod it!' he said. 'What do nets matter?'

Zoot and I spent most of Saturday morning wandering about town looking for something for David. It wasn't till we hit the flea market, where as a rule only junk is to be found, that we unearthed the perfect present: a print, a real, genuine, Victorian print, of fox terriers. What made it perfect was that one of them looked just like Max . . .

All we had to do then was go to Boots and buy a frame. We chose one that could either hang on the wall or be stood up by itself, so that while he was in hospital he could put it on his locker and when he came home, if he wanted, he could put it over the bed. Max being one of the dearest objects in his life, second only to

Abbey (and then only just), we reckoned that over the bed was probably where he'd want it.

We ate lunch at Larry's, where we framed the print and wrote a card to go with it, then took it out to Glenthorne Avenue to give to Abbey. Abbey wasn't there. Her mother said she was 'up in town', meaning London.

'What on earth is she doing up there?' I said.

Mrs Johnson said she didn't know, Abbey hadn't told her.

'Just said that she was going. I didn't like to pry. Things being what they are . . . have you two young folk had lunch?'

We said that we had and that really we ought to be on our way, but somehow she managed to get us inside; and once inside it was very difficult to say no to a cup of coffee. She really seemed to need us there. What it was, we discovered, she wanted to talk about David. She couldn't talk about him with Abbey, she said: Abbey just closed up like a clam.

'I hardly dare even mention his name.'

We stayed for almost twenty minutes; that was as much as we could take. Mrs Johnson is such a worrier, she just didn't seem able to grasp about being positive. I could quite understand how it was that Abbey wouldn't let her talk. Zoot and I felt really down when we got out.

'She's pretty old,' said Zoot. 'I guess being negative's probably easier than being positive when you get to that age.'

Sunday evening Abbey rang, as she had promised. She said that she had been to see David, and had given him our love, and had given him the print, and—

'How is he?' I said. I had to interrupt her because

just for a minute it seemed as though she was going to go racing on ahead without telling me.

Abbey said, as she had said before, that he was 'all right'.

'Just so long as you're being positive,' I said.

She assured me that she was, but when I asked her if she'd told David about the girl who climbed mountains she admitted that she hadn't; not yet. She said she hadn't thought it was quite the right moment. I couldn't understand her. *I* would have talked about it. It's one of the very first things I would have talked about. If I had been David, lying there in bed, I would have liked the thought of being able to climb mountains.

'Yes,' said Abbey, when I told her this, 'but you're different.'

She didn't say how I was different. Perhaps she meant that I was more ebullient (for ebullient read obnoxious: once at my junior school some of the girls started a society for the crushing of Robyn Mather. I can't imagine anyone would ever have started a society for the crushing of David.)

'Anyway,' I said, steering the conversation back to a more positive course, 'he liked the print?'

Abbey said yes, he did. 'It sort of upset him, but he thought it was super.'

'Up*set* him?' I said.

'Well, you know . . . made him think of Max. He keeps asking about him.'

I didn't like to think of our print upsetting David. Upsetting people wasn't at all a positive sort of thing to do. Abbey sighed and said she supposed that people were more easily upset after having had operations than at other times, but that maybe soon he would be allowed to go home and then he would be able to see

79

Max for himself. We both of us agreed that it would be very *positive* for David to be able to go home and see Max.

I tried asking Abbey what she had been doing yesterday, up in town all by herself, but she just said evasively that she would 'tell me'.

'Let's meet up and go into school together tomorrow . . . eight thirty your bus stop. Shall we?'

I said yes, OK, fine. It was years since Abbey and I had met up at the bus stop and gone into school together. I know of course why she wanted to do it tomorrow: tomorrow was the day when Mr Francis was going to tell the sixth year about David. She obviously felt the need of my support at such a time. I didn't begrudge it her.

Abbey looked extraordinarily purposeful when I met her on Monday. Like someone who has suddenly discovered her mission in life. She told me what she had been doing on Saturday, up in town: she had been sitting in the medical section of the Marylebone Public Library, 'reading about David' . . . What she hadn't been able to read on the spot she had carried away with her, four vasty tomes (I saw them, later) back to Clearhaven, to read in the privacy of her bedroom. She had spent all day Sunday, when she hadn't been visiting David, doing nothing but read.

'I just felt that I had to *know*.'

And so she had ploughed through all these dry-as-dust texts, all full of statistics and medical terms which she couldn't understand and had to keep checking out (I would have just skipped over them: not Abbey). Now she seemed to know almost as much as Pop; maybe even more. She kept telling me, as we walked, all about these new drugs—'cocktails', she called them—so many mg of this, so many mg of that, some

80

that had to be given intravenously, some that were taken by mouth, and what you did, you had to balance them, you had to keep monitoring them, because some by themselves would be toxic, so what you had to do—

I listened, in awed silence, as she rattled it all off. They all seemed to have such pretty names, those horrible drugs. There was one, I remember, called Christine (*Christine?* Can it have been, really?) one that sounded like Adrian, another that I thought had something to do with lemons. As a result of her reading, Abbey told me, she was much happier. She felt now, she said, that she could cope: now she knew what it was they were fighting. And that it was something that *could* be fought.

'Because these drugs, you know, Robyn, have quite altered the picture. The prognosis is far better now than it used to be.'

I wasn't quite sure what a prognosis was (I asked Pop later and he said, 'outlook'). All I knew was that Abbey was being positive, and that if she were positive it would help David to be so. I didn't start bleating about drugs making your hair fall out. I felt ashamed that anything so petty could still bother me.

At school we found Zoot, hovering outside the common room. He had obviously been lying in wait for us.

'Guess what? The Wingbag's had a sudden attack of the humanities . . . we don't have to go in there'—he jerked his head towards the common room—'if we don't want.'

I looked instinctively at Abbey for guidance. I would actually, for all my socializing instincts, have preferred not; but if Abbey decided that we should—

'I think we ought,' she said.

She said afterwards that she felt it was our duty—being David's friends, and therefore, in a manner of speaking, his representatives. Abbey is always very strong on what she conceives as duty. I didn't exactly see it myself, and I'm not certain that Zoot did, either, but we wouldn't have let Abbey go in on her own.

We sat at the back, in a row, perched on the window sill, while the rest of the sixth draped themselves in armchairs or squatted on table tops or leaned up against the wall, plainly wondering what it was all about and why they had been told to gather there. Most of them probably thought there was going to be a drugs bust (quite a few *were* on pot, though I don't think anything stronger) or else a crackdown of some kind, like the previous year when local residents had complained of contraceptives littering the edge of the playing field and Mr Francis had risen up in wrath and said that if we were going to behave like sex maniacs we could damned well go and do it elsewhere, he wasn't having any school of *his* gain a reputation as a knocking shop.

Somebody, while we were waiting—I think it was Pilch—I *bet* it was Pilch—blew off this really loud raspberry. There was a ripple of giggles, accompanied by the usual jeering and catcalls; and then, into the midst of it, came the Windbag's voice: '*SHUT UP!*' It was the shortest sentence I'd ever heard him speak.

I think they sussed, then, that this was going to be something more than just an ordinary bawling out. They all fell silent, and Whingeing Osborne, squashed against the lockers (he was the sort who always got squashed against something) swivelled his head towards the three of us, perched on our window sill, as if trying to glean from our faces whether we might know something that the rest of them did not. Abbey sat aloof, hands folded in her lap, eyes focused on some point in the far distance. Zoot, leaning back into the angle of the window, was hugging his knee and chewing on a piece of gum, doing his best to have no part in the proceedings. I, like an idiot, caught Whinge's eye—but only for a second. Mr Francis came in almost immediately and Whinge snapped to attention. He didn't look at us again. Nobody did.

'Right,' said Mr Francis. 'If everybody's here—'

He kept it mercifully brief; just gave the bare facts and nothing more, though I could see that that was enough for most people. More than enough for some. Quite a few of the girls went noticeably pale, whilst others turned bright pink and looked as if they might be going to cry. Pilch looked uncomfortable, and Whingeing Osborne's Adam's apple bounced up and down a few times in his scrawny neck. Whether out of embarrassment or consideration for our feelings they were all very careful to avoid looking at us, either then or afterwards, though they didn't get much of a chance afterwards because Mr Francis kept the three of us back for a little fatherly chat. I can't remember much about it now. All I remember is him saying that we were 'very young' to have to face such an ordeal, and me thinking that David was very young, too, which perhaps showed in my face because he instantly added that of course it was far worse for David and that as his closest friends we bore a great burden of responsibility. And I remember, at that point, it all threatened to get a bit heavy, with Mr Francis placing a hand on Abbey's shoulder and saying, 'Don't ever hesitate to seek help if you feel that it's becoming too much for you,' which nearly went and cracked her up (after all her brave resolutions). Still,

I'm sure Mr Francis handled it as well as anyone could.

It was later, in assembly, when he asked the school to offer up prayers, that he made his mistake. Not that he could have known; how could he have done? Even I didn't realize, to begin with. I remember hearing Abbey, at my side, draw in her breath with a sharp hiss. I remember glancing at her, but not really thinking anything of it, until quite suddenly, without the least warning, bang in the middle of 'David, our brother,' she shot to her feet and went hurtling from the hall. I remember Zoot looking round at me in alarm—me dithering as to whether or not I should go after her—and then, out of the corner of my eye, seeing Willie start up. That was when I stopped dithering. I remember leaping out ahead of her and hurling myself at the nearest exit, prepared to barge if necessary. Anything to keep Willie from getting there first. Nobody in their right mind could possibly want *Willie* at a time like this.

'Abbey!' I pelted in pursuit of her down the corridor. She was several blocks ahead of me, she had almost reached the far exit leading to the field, but she stopped when she realized who it was; stopped and turned, eyes blazing, facing me head-on.

'What's wrong?' I said.

She threw her hair back over her shoulders.

'I can't take all that fucking crap!'

It shook me, Abbey using language like that. It was like the Queen telling someone to get stuffed, or a nun shrieking 'shit!' in the street.

'Abbey!' I said. 'It's only *prayers*.'

'Prayers?' She spat it at me as if it were a dirty word. 'It's an insult! It's an insult to David! You know he doesn't believe in that sort of garbage! You know what he said—what he said—' Rage was so choking her

84

she could hardly get the words out. 'That time—about funerals—none of that religious crap! And now they're doing it! It's a mockery! It's a sham!'

'Not to them,' I said. 'Not if they believe in it.'

'They don't believe in it! They just mouth it like so much mumbo jumbo! That's all it is, anyway . . . meaningless crud!'

'Abbey—' I pawed at her, nervously. This bawling termagant wasn't the Abbey that I knew. 'Abbey, it's not worth getting so worked up about! Really it isn't!'

She reared up, angrily, shying away from me.

'What isn't? David's health isn't? You don't think that's something I should get worked up about? His *life* could be at stake! And then you tell me not to get worked up . . . *Jesus!*'

'But Abbey, they *care*,' I said. 'They're just expressing it in a different way. Even if it is mumbo jumbo—well, there could be *some*thing in it. The power of prayer—'

'Don't go on to me about *prayer*!' screamed Abbey. 'It's not prayer that's going to save him, you idiot!' She hauled at the door. 'It's medicine!'

This time, I let her go. There didn't seem any point my chasing after her: I obviously wasn't saying anything that helped.

On my way back down the corridor I crossed paths with Willie. We didn't speak. Willie just pointed silently, questioningly, in the direction of the door: I nodded. Abbey, I figured, would have to take her chance.

6

Abbey apologized to me later.

'I didn't mean to yell at you . . . I just felt I was going mad. I felt as if my head was going to burst. As if—'

'It's all right,' I said. 'Honestly.'

She didn't have to explain. I was remembering what Mumps had said about being prepared to make allowances. I knew now what she meant: even Abbey, controlled, disciplined, sensible Abbey, could go to pieces under pressure.

'What is so awful,' she said, 'is the way everything else just suddenly seems so trivial.'

Out there in the world terrible, terrible things were happening . . . but Abbey's own, personal world had shrunk to a pinpoint. Yesterday she had been worried about the bomb and nuclear waste and radiation: today all she could think about was David.

'Well, but that's how it should be,' I said. 'You can only worry about one thing at a time.'

'Yes,' said Abbey. She sighed. 'That's what Willie said . . . there's only a limited amount that each of us can handle. You just have to take things in order of priority.'

'Willie said that?'

Abbey nodded.

'She was really nice. Really sympathetic. I'm going round to have tea with her next Thursday.'

Tea with Willie! Well, I thought, whatever turns you on. (The truth was, I suppose, that I was jealous.)

'I was wondering'—Abbey hesitated—'I was wondering whether you and Zoot would like to go and see David?'

86

'Does he want us to?' I said. 'I mean . . . has he asked?'

Abbey admitted that he hadn't—but then, she said, he hadn't really asked for anyone.

'Only Max.' She gave a little laugh; apologetic, almost. 'He's the only one he really wants.' There was a pause. 'But I'm sure he *would* like to see you.'

'Well, so long as you're sure,' I said. 'I wouldn't want to go barging in where I'm not welcome.'

'Oh, *no!*' said Abbey. She sounded shocked. 'You wouldn't ever not be welcome.'

Everybody, following Mr Francis' talk, was bending over backwards to be tactful. Nobody ever mentioned David when Abbey was around, nobody intruded upon her with questions. It was as if they sensed she wasn't the sort to gain relief from talking and might well misinterpret normal friendly concern as nosiness or prying. I was the one they turned to for that. I was the one they asked their questions of, and I didn't mind, because unlike Abbey I find it helps to discuss things. I told them everything I could; everything that I knew and that Pop had told me. And although one couldn't help suspecting that one or two of them, notably Whinge, were just being ghoulish, most people, you could tell, had been genuinely shaken by the news. Abbey said tartly that they were just scared 'in case it happens to them'.

It wasn't like Abbey to be sour, but Abbey, these days, definitely wasn't herself. I knew I had to make allowances for her, and I did try, though it wasn't always easy. Apart from anything else I was never certain how much she really needed me. Quite often, instead of seeking me out during the breaks so that we could walk round the field together, or sit together

87

in the canteen, which is what we would normally have done, she'd just disappear without telling me and I'd only discover afterwards that she'd been having an extra study session or had 'gone to talk to Willie'.

Since Zoot spent every spare minute he could in the nets it meant that I was left very much to my own devices. After a bit I took to going around with the two Janes. Little Jane (Waters) had been a friend of mine in Brownies, back in the days before I started at Clareville. She was also playing the part of Hero in *Much Ado*, and as Big Jane was stage managing we spent quite a lot of our time discussing the play and going over lines. Now and again Pilch would join us. He had, inevitably, taken over as Benedick. I resented it like mad to begin with. Pilch himself obviously felt bad about it because he came up to me after the first rehearsal and said, 'I did want to play Benedick, but I wouldn't have had it happen this way. Not for the world. Honestly.'

It was difficult, after that, to go on resenting. Besides, although I would never in a million years have confessed it to Abbey, Pilch actually was a far better actor than David. I asked him one day why he'd never taken part in any of the shows before, and he said that he had, 'back at the beginning'.

'Yes, but only small parts,' I said, remembering. 'Why never anything big?'

Pilch just shrugged, and left it to me to work out. It took me some time to stumble upon the truth: the truth being, plainly and simply, that Pilch had always been overlooked in favour of David.

Quite soon, Pilch and I and the two Janes had made up a sort of foursome. (Only temporary: only until David was back and things returned to normal.) We started spending most of our lunch breaks together, sitting on the field going over lines, rehearsing the odd scene. Once, when Pilch and I were doing one of our Beatrice–Benedick bits, Whingeing Osborne turned up to watch.

'Not bad,' he said, at the end. (Whinge always fancied himself as something of a drama critic, although he never to my knowledge actually risked getting up on stage himself.) 'I said right from the start they ought to cast you as Benedick.'

Pilch frowned, and muttered something.

'You don't want to be bashful,' said Whinge. 'That's what it's all about, isn't it?' He turned to me for confirmation. 'The acting business? That's the way to get on.'

'What is?' I said, coldly.

'Well . . . stepping into other people's shoes. An accepted fact of life, isn't it?'

It may have been—but he didn't have to *say* so. It really upset Pilch.

'Look,' he said urgently, as soon as Whinge was out of earshot, 'if there's any chance of David getting back in time to take over—'

'Oh, Pilch, don't be daft!' I said.

A hurt look crossed his face.

'You were the one that said it wouldn't matter if Benedick walked with a limp! You were the one—'

'I didn't mean that,' I said. 'I meant . . . the part's yours. You might just as well make the most of it.'

Sometimes, rehearsing *Much Ado*, playing tennis, going to fencing classes (I fenced with Pilch. I would have fenced with Zoot, but he had dropped out, being too much preoccupied with his precious cricket, and Abbey, too, had fallen by the wayside), sometimes I found that for quite long stretches I would almost forget about David. Well—not really *forget*; I was always very well aware, just below the surface, of the fact that he wasn't with us; but at least not consciously agonizing, as I'm sure that Abbey was.

I always felt guilty when I realized this. I would think, 'How can I possibly be *enjoying* myself when David is shut away in hospital?' I felt like some kind of monster. How could I be so *selfish*? I spoke to Zoot about it once, and he said that he, too, sometimes half forgot and then suffered terrible pangs of conscience as a result. And then I was so foul to Abbey one time. It still causes me grief to remember. I'd just come from a fencing class, all flushed with success because I'd scored three hits against Pilch, who usually beat me hands down, when I came across Abbey, wandering like a ghost along the corridor.

'Ha ha!' I cried; and crouched into the on-guard position. 'Have at thee, varlet!'

Abbey smiled, rather wanly.

'Where've you been?' I said. 'Not closeted with Willie again?'

'No, I've been talking to Barney about the rounders.'

'Oh, yes! The rounders.' In my excitement over everything else, I had almost forgotten about it. 'How are we doing for sponsors?'

'All right. But I don't think that I shall be playing.'

'Why not?' I swished with my foil. It would be a tremendous advantage, when I got to drama school, to have already done a year's fencing. 'You can't not play, you're the one that's organizing it!'

'Oh, I'll still organize,' said Abbey.

'So why not play?' Not that Abbey is necessarily the world's greatest, but she is certainly above average; and anyway, that was beside the point. It had been her idea, she couldn't chicken out now.

'I don't feel that it's right,' said Abbey. She pressed her lips together. 'Not if David can't.'

'But that's crazy! I'm sure if you asked him he'd say he wants you to.'

'I don't expect,' said Abbey, and there was a little tremor in her voice, 'that he would care one way or the other.'

Oh, heavens! I thought. Not the tragedy queen bit. (I actually *did* think that. It's quite one of the horridest things that I have ever thought and is something I shall never forgive myself for.)

'So if David doesn't care,' I said, 'why should you?'

I remember—I shall always remember—the wounded expression that came into Abbey's eyes.

'There is such a thing as loyalty,' she said.

That was the point at which I was really foul. The shadow of Abbey's unhappiness was threatening my own little patch of euphoria and I suppose, if the truth is to be told, I resented it.

'For goodness' sake,' I snapped. 'Life has to go on!'

Of course I felt dreadful about it afterwards, but by then it was too late. What had been said had been said; I couldn't take it back. I felt so dreadful that I inwardly projected my self-hatred on to the unsuspecting Whinge. I remember looking at the back of his pimply neck in English and thinking that if anyone had to be mutilated, why couldn't it be him? He was such a loathsome little toad, what difference could it make? Even if he died, nobody would miss him. Subsequently I felt a bit dreadful about that, too, because after all it wasn't Whinge's fault, and maybe, just maybe, there might be people who would be sorry if he went—parents, maybe; brothers, sisters. But I only felt a little bit dreadful and it very quickly passed, whereas I have felt dreadful about Abbey ever since.

If I didn't in so many words apologize to her, as she, earlier, had apologized to me, it was because it was almost too deep for apology. I went up to her at the end of the day and said, 'Ab?' And I slipped my arm through hers and squeezed her wrist with my fingers, and she let me do it and didn't cringe or pull away, which was quite unusual because Abbey has never been physically demonstrative. Only with David. With everyone else she's always been quite shy.

'Which was the night,' I said, 'that you were going to Willie's?'

Abbey reminded me: Thursday.

'That's tomorrow!'

She nodded.

'Did you ask David if he'd like to see us?'

'Yes. I think he would.'

'So we'll go,' I said, 'shall we?'

'Would you?' said Abbey. She made it sound as though we were doing her a favour.

'Look,' I said, 'all we've been waiting for is an invitation . . .'

We went the next night, Zoot and I. We were the only ones there. David's parents, Abbey said, had decided it would be more tactful if they were to stay away: that David would be happier alone with 'just his friends'. I don't know if it would have been any better had they come; I suppose it could have been worse, though I tend to feel that there is safety in numbers.

It wasn't a good visit. Zoot and I (we didn't discuss it: we didn't have to) were both shaken by the change that had taken place in David. I don't mean physically, I think we might have been prepared for that. In fact, I had been bracing myself for it, telling myself firmly

92

that whatever one did one must be careful not to betray any sense of shock. Well, physically, there wasn't any shock, because to all outward appearances David was just the same as he had always been, apart from a bit of hospital pallor through having been shut away from the outside world for so long. I mean, one knew—all too well one knew—what had been done to him, but one shut one's mind to that, one simply didn't think about it. The David sitting up in bed seemed no different from the David with whom we had laughed and joked and had fun all these years.

But he was different. He wasn't laughing any more, or responding to our jokes. I told him a joke I'd been storing up specially, about this man who lost his camel and went to the police to report it, and—well, I won't tell it here as it's rather rude, but it is actually quite funny. Pilch had laughed at it. David did his best, he pretended to laugh, because it's only polite when people tell you a joke and he always had nice manners, but it was very obvious that he *was* only pretending; that it was quite an effort for him even to do that. I might have put it down to my lack of skill as a joke-teller, but then Zoot had a go, with something *really* disgusting, and not even he could raise more than the faintest and most fleeting of smiles.

We tried talking about school, telling him incidents that had occurred, bits of gossip (such as the rumour going round that Whinge and Jammy Wilson were having an affair, the special piquancy of this being that Jammy Wilson, who taught junior maths, was generally suspected of being a transvestite—or T/V as Zoot and David would persist in shortening it to) but we both knew that we weren't really engaging his attention, save on the most superficial level. Things that happened at school didn't seem to be of interest to

93

him any more. Nor things that happened out-side—outside school, that is. Outside school, outside the hospital. I told him about a CND meeting I'd been to with Abbey: David said he reckoned CND was a waste of time. Zoot then tried discussing the test match: he didn't even know what the latest score was. I could see that that really shook Zoot. The look that he sent me, across the bed, signalled quite plainly, *something is wrong here.*

I decided it was about time that I started being positive: we couldn't sit here negatively for the next half-hour.

'So when are you coming back?' I said. I said it very briskly to show that I meant business.

'Don't know,' said David.

'Haven't they said?' Pop had told me it would probably be another week or two, so they could complete the first course of treatment while David was still in hospital. 'They must have given you *some* idea?'

He hunched a shoulder.

'Next month, maybe.'

'You don't sound exactly overjoyed at the prospect!'

'What is there to be overjoyed about?'

'Well—'

Zoot sent me a warning glance. It seemed to say: tread carefully. But one either says things or one doesn't.

'Have they started you on physiotherapy yet?'

David grunted.

'So how often d'you have to go?'

'Every poxy flaming day.'

'But that's good! The more you do, the sooner you'll be mobile again.' (I said mobile because it sounded better than 'walking'. It was an expression that I had picked up from Pop.) 'Did Abbey tell you about that

94

girl that climbs mountains?'

David said no, she hadn't. He didn't say it at all encouragingly but I pressed ahead, anyway. After all, *some*one had to be positive.

'There's this girl,' I said, 'who had a leg off' (Zoot winced) 'and now she's going on these climbing expeditions up places like Mount Everest and —what's that other one?'

'South face of the Eiger?' said David. He gave a short laugh.

'Not the Eiger,' I said. 'I think it began with an M—'

'A molehill?'

'A what? No! Somewhere like—what's the name of another mountain? The Matterhorn! Maybe it was the Matterhorn. Could it have been the Matterhorn? Or was it—'

Zoot said, 'Belt up, Robyn! Boring on about mountains. Who wants to climb the flaming stupid things anyway?'

'This girl,' I said. 'She—'

'Shut it,' said Zoot. 'Hey!' He poked a finger into David's ribs. 'Did I tell you about Andy Pandy? Apparently, he went off to Brighton, all by himself—'

I listened, impatiently. Telling stories about Andy! How was that supposed to help? David also listened, but with an air of detachment, as if Zoot were relating things that had happened in another world—another universe. Nothing to do with him. You might almost have thought that he had never heard of a person called Andy, nor ever been to the place that was Brighton. I had the feeling it would have been the same whoever or whatever we had talked about.

When I got home that night Mumps said, 'So how is he?' It was what I had kept saying to Abbey: 'How is he?' And she had replied, 'He's all right.' I suppose I should have known, when she said that, that he wasn't. Mumps obviously sensed that something was amiss.

'Not too good?' she said.

I hastened to explain that he was all right *physically*—'I mean, he is, isn't he?' I looked at her in sudden terror. 'There's nothing else? Nothing you're keeping from us?'

She reassured me.

'But Pop would tell you, wouldn't he?' I insisted. 'If the hospital told him, he'd tell you?'

'Robyn, darling, I really can't say,' said Mumps. 'All I can promise you, and I *do* promise you, is that I personally am not keeping anything hidden.'

She added that if David seemed withdrawn it was hardly to be wondered at: 'You can't expect someone to go through an experience like that and emerge unscathed. Things are bound to be a bit bumpy just at first. He has to come to terms with a whole new concept of himself.'

I saw that; but still it worried me that he wasn't being *positive*. I discussed it with Abbey next morning at school, and she confessed what she hadn't told me before, that she had almost given up trying to be positive when she was with him.

'He just doesn't seem to care.'

'But that's terrible!' I said.

'I know,' said Abbey. She looked at me, piteously. 'But what can one do?'

There had to be something. I wrestled with the problem all that day, during English, when I should have been concentrating on W.H. Auden, during fencing, when I let Pilch run circles round me, during rounders (practice for The Match) when I disgraced myself dropping three catches in a row, until I finally came up with a solution: a Plan. Zoot was horrified when I put it to him.

'Take *Max*? Are you out of your tree?'

I didn't think I was. I thought it was an excellent idea; I was very proud of it. Psychologically, it seemed to me, it was just what David needed. I had remembered Abbey saying how 'Max was the only one he really wanted'. Saying how our print had upset him (even though he thought it was super) because it made him think of Max: how he kept asking after him. I remembered how she and I had both agreed that for David to be able to go home and see Max in the flesh would be something that was extremely positive. Well, David couldn't go home just yet, he still had another couple of weeks before they would let him out; so if David couldn't go to Max I reckoned Max would have to be brought to David.

'It's Mahomet and the mountain,' I said, 'isn't it?'

Zoot said he didn't know anything about flaming Mahomet (so much for the Windbag and his comparative religions) and for crying out loud don't start on about mountains again.

'Flaming mountains, flaming dogs . . . they don't allow flaming dogs in hospitals!'

I said that I was perfectly well aware of that, thank you. (It does make me so mad when people niggle and nitpick.)

'So how are you proposing to get him in there? Tie him in a sack?'

I said that it was perfectly simple: I would go in and see David, while Zoot handed Max through the window. Zoot's jaw dropped open. (*Idiot.*)

'You're bonkers,' he said.

'I am not bonkers, I'm trying to do something to help David! For heaven's sake!' I stamped a foot. I was really getting quite angry. 'What do you suggest? We just stand by and do nothing? There's only one way of fighting this thing and that's to have a positive attitude towards it. How can David have a positive attitude if he's just lying there brooding? You stopped me trying to talk to him about it, telling him all that junk he didn't want to hear. The *least* you can do now is help me restore his reason for living.'

That, actually, was a phrase I had recently read in a *Reader's Digest* story (about a woman who had looked death in the face and lived to tell the tale). I had thought at the time that it was rather corny, but it rattled Zoot. It was meant to rattle him: I was in earnest about this.

'What David needs is to be brought out of himself, otherwise he'll just give up and let the thing take over. *We*'ve tried, Abbey's tried, Max is the only thing that's left . . . I mean, it can't do any harm, and it *could* do a lot of good.'

Zoot still—he made it obvious—thought the whole scheme was harebrained. He would still, really and truly, have preferred to play no part in it; but he cared about David and he did agree with me that something needed to be done.

We laid our plans very carefully. (We didn't tell Abbey: we both felt, instinctively, it was better she shouldn't know.) Point number one, we would need to be at the hospital at a time when David was not going to have any other visitors. Since his parents and Abbey went every night, and also at weekends, that meant a weekday afternoon—which meant cutting classes and probably getting into an almighty row afterwards, but we neither of us cared about that. We decided for the following Monday, on the grounds that Monday afternoons we had a session with the

Windbag; also, as Zoot said, if we were going to do the deed then 'why piss about? Let's get it over with.' I agreed. It seemed to me the sooner David could be induced to start thinking positively the better.

Point number two was a more tricky one: how to get hold of Max? We could hardly expect David's mother to endorse our proposed action.

'Can't really blame her,' said Zoot, 'can you?'

'Look, just shut up,' I said, 'and stop wittering!'

We racked our brains for some plausible excuse for needing to borrow a fox terrier for the day—'Project for school?' 'Taking him to the beach?'—but they all sounded far too contrived to be true. In the end, I said we would just have to kidnap him.

There was a silence, then: 'How?' said Zoot.

'Oh—' I waved a hand. It didn't seem to me that it would be too difficult. In warm weather Max would be almost bound to be out of doors—and almost bound to be with his soul mate, Sable. He always spent his time with Sable when David wasn't around. David himself had told me that. They were great buddies, he had said, Max and Sable. We had only to pick our moment, steal round to the back of the house, make our way to the paddock—

'And then what?'

Then we grabbed Max and ran. Nothing to it!

'That's what you always say,' grumbled Zoot.

On my way in to school on Monday morning I stopped off at a pet shop and bought a nylon dog lead and a Bonio, which I hid in my briefcase; then at midday we did what Zoot called 'a runner', slipping out of school by one of the side gates and making it to the bus station just in time to snatch a quick couple of sandwiches before catching the bus which would take us out to David's place. It's a forty-minute journey out there, and then at the other end there's a long stretch of main road plus about half a mile of lane before the farm is reached, so we knew we didn't have any time to waste. Afternoon visiting was from 2.30 till 3.30 and the buses only ran once every hour: we were aiming for the 1.20 back into town and we couldn't afford to miss it.

The most dangerous part of the proceedings, as far as I was concerned, was walking down the lane—if we bumped into anyone coming the other way we were done for. I wanted to try cutting cross country but Zoot said that it would take too long. He said we'd just have to keep our eyes peeled and be prepared to dive into the ditch. I can't say that the idea appealed (you never know what might be lurking in ditches) but I thought of David as he had been last Thursday, all troubled and turned in on himself, and I knew that this was not a time for worrying about mud or rotting carcasses.

Fortunately no dive into the ditch was necessary. We reached the end of the lane and both farm and farm-house looked deserted. Cautiously we crept across the yard, through the gaggle of geese and ducks, past Bertie the goat on the end of his rope tether, past the rotting hulk of tractor, which David said had been there ever since he was a toddler—it was almost totally overgrown, now, by weeds—and through the gate on to the public footpath, bounded shoulder-high by cow parsley. Above the cow parsley the fields stretched out like a great golden sea to the horizon. Not a soul in sight; only, in the distance, a vehicle that bounced and bumped over a rutted track. Zoot, shading his eyes, said that it was a Land Rover and that it was moving away from us. David's father, probably. (David had sometimes borrowed the

Land Rover to take us down to Brighton. How long would it be, I wondered, before he could do that again?)

'Come on!' Zoot jerked his head. 'Let's move it!'

Stealthily, under cover of the cow parsley, we made our way along the footpath, at the end of which was the field where Sable was kept, with the two donkeys, Annabelle and Lisa. We saw Sable almost immediately: he was standing in the shade, beneath the oak tree, with the donkeys at his side. At first I thought Max wasn't there, and my heart sank, because if he was in the house not even I would be bold enough to make a kidnap attempt; and if he had gone hunting, we hadn't a hope of locating him. I told Zoot to do David's special whistle, fingers in the mouth (which I can't do no matter how hard I practise. Zoot always used to jeer and say, 'Women's lib? Don't make me laugh!'). Instantly, to my relief, a pointed nose came quivering out of the hut where Sable and the donkeys take shelter in cold weather. I called, 'Maxie? Here, boy! Good boy! Bikkie!' which is the sort of silly baby talk which seems to work wonders with dogs. Or perhaps he just smelt the biscuits, or thought that as we were friends of David, David himself could not be far away. Whichever it was, he came running. I grabbed him and hoicked him over the gate and said, 'Good boy! There's a boy! Come find Davie,' slipped him on his lead, showed him his biscuit, and then we were away, running like stags, back across the farmyard (goat, geese and ducks all turned their heads to stare), up the lane, along the road, and there was the bus, making its way towards us. Triumphant, as we collapsed into the nearest seat, I thumped Zoot on the shoulder.

'Told you it'd be easy!'

Zoot just grunted and said the most difficult part was yet to come.

Nobody stopped us as we walked through the hospital gates. One or two people looked a bit askance at Max on his lead, but nobody actually said anything.

'Don't see why they should,' I said. 'There's no notices about dogs not being allowed into the grounds . . . can *you* see any notices about dogs not being allowed into the grounds?'

Zoot said that he couldn't, and told me not to shout. I said that I wasn't shouting, just projecting my voice quite normally, but Zoot by now was definitely nervous. Part of the trouble was, he's not really a dog person. I suggested, if he liked, that he could go in and see David and I would take charge of Max, but that only made him even more agitated. He said we should go and have a bit of a scout round before I went in, so we set off down the path which led to Maternity, Haematology and Christy Wing, which was where David was. We managed to locate the windows of Humphrey Spencer ward, but couldn't work out which one was closest to David's bed. We narrowed it down to two, and Zoot said that he would position himself between them and await my signal.

'Just don't leave it too long . . . I feel a right prat.'

'Don't be so silly!' I said. 'There's nobody to see you.'

The windows were too high off the ground for anyone inside to catch sight of him unless they actually went up and peered out—which of course they well might, but as I said, so what? He was only standing there with a small-sized dog on the end of a lead. He wasn't *doing* anything.

Zoot said gloomily, 'Not till I start stuffing him through the window.' He really was *very* chicken-hearted. I wouldn't have expected it, of Zoot.

102

He was going to need something to stand on, so between us we dragged over one of the benches that were dotted about the lawn. The one we chose had a plaque saying that it had been donated by Sylvia Cleary, 'In Gratitude'. We parked it midway between the two windows and I instructed Zoot to sit there and await my summons and to stop Max from barking.

'Just so long as he doesn't try screwing me,' said Zoot, darkly.

Zoot had a real hang-up about that. Once on the beach Max had taken a fancy to one of his feet. The rest of us had laughed like drains, but Zoot had been quite put out. Felt it was compromising his masculinity, no doubt. He had told David that his dog was 'a flaming foot fetishist'. (But the point, as David had said, was what had Zoot been *doing* with his foot?)

I left him sitting there, looking decidedly ill at ease (with Max happily cocking his leg against the side of the bench) whilst I went back along the path to the main entrance. It was twenty minutes into visiting time but obviously not many people came on a Monday afternoon for Humphrey Spencer was practically empty: all the nurses locked away in their cubby hole and scarcely a visitor in sight. There weren't all that many patients in sight, either. I realized that a lot of them, those that were what Pop called ambulatory, had gone into the day room to watch television or play cards, and I thought that that was good, because the fewer people about the better.

One of the patients from David's cubicle had gone off to the day room, the other two, both elderly men, appeared to be asleep. David himself was sitting out of bed, in a chair, which disconcerted me; partly because I hadn't expected it, partly because—well, partly just *because*. It embarrassed me a bit, I suppose. Made me not know where to look. David was obviously a bit thrown. He said, 'Robyn! What are you doing here?'

'I came to see you,' I said. And then: 'You're out of bed!'

'Yes.'

There was a pause.

'Does it bother you?' said David.

'Bother me? No! I mean—no! It's just—I hadn't realized—'

David gave me such a funny look.

'Hadn't realized what?' he said.

'I hadn't realized that they let you get up.'

'Oh.' He seemed abruptly to lose interest. 'Some big deal.'

'Well—yes. I mean . . . I knew you went to physio—'

'Yes, I hop there,' said David. 'Quite a feat—or do I mean foot? Ha ha! That's a joke. You may laugh.'

I smiled, uncertainly.

'You ought to try telling it to Zoot,' said David. 'It sounds like his sort of thing.'

'Zoot's outside,' I said.

'What's he doing out there? Got cold feet? Note I said f—'

Not another foot joke; I couldn't take it.

'David, listen!' I said. 'I've got a surprise for you!'

'Oh?' He looked at me, warily. (I don't altogether blame him: I'd have probably looked at me pretty warily, too.)

'It's outside. Just hang on a sec—'

I darted across to the window and peered down. Zoot was still there, sitting as I had left him, on Sylvia Cleary, with Max sitting bolt upright beside him, good as gold. I waved a hand: Zoot saw me, and waved back.

104

'What are you doing?' said David.

'Trying—' I tugged—'to open'—tug—'the window!'

The window shot skywards with a crash. One of the old men stirred slightly, the other didn't move. David was staring at me as if I had run mad. But then he ought to be used to my madness by now: he had once told me that I was a raving bananas case.

Outside I saw Zoot heaving at Sylvia Cleary, trying to get her in position. Max, at the end of his lead, was bouncing joyously up and down, eager, as always, to participate. Boing! boing! boing! He was like a creature on springs. I saw him rebound off Zoot's shoulder and Zoot trip over the lead and bash his shin against the edge of Sylvia Cleary and Max, growing hysterical, race round in a circle, pinning Zoot's legs together, and I knew a moment of sudden misgiving and wondered if I had done the right thing. I had this vision of an uncontrolled Max coming hurtling in through the window, making a beeline for David, knocking him off balance, causing havoc and disaster. I had visions of stitches being torn out and arteries bursting open and me being responsible for it all.

'David!' I said, urgently. 'You couldn't get back into bed, could you?'

'What for?' he said.

Below the window, Zoot had finally managed to get Sylvia Cleary in position. He was just about to step up on to her. I turned, and rushed at David; and in that moment, Max barked.

I can only assume that dog-owners recognize the barks of their own dogs just as mothers (so they *say*) can recognize the cries of their own babies. David stiffened. He shot a look towards the window; then back, searchingly, at me.

105

'David, *please*,' I said.

Without a word, he began to lever himself back to bed. As he did so, Max barked again, shriller this time, more excited. I guessed that either he had got wind of David or that Zoot, like an idiot, had gone and told him. (Zoot doesn't actually believe that you *can* tell dogs things, but of course you can.)

'Robyn, you're crazy!' said David.

'Yes, I know,' I said; and at the last minute I snatched up a pillow from the empty bed and thrust it at him.

Zoot's head, now, was at the window. I dashed across.

'Take him!' said Zoot.

I don't know if you have ever tried to contain an over-excited fox terrier, especially one that can see its owner only a few yards away and is desperate to get at him. I did my best, but Max did better: with a scream of sheer joy, he plunged out of my arms and hurled himself at David. Slap, boing, wallop, right into the middle of the bed. (It was fortunate I'd thought about the pillow.) The next second and they were hugging each other, Max with his front paws wrapped round David's neck, his tail going like a windmill, tongue lolloping great wet licks all over David's nose and cheeks and chin and just wherever it could reach, and David clasping Max in his arms and laughing and crying both at the same time and saying, 'Max! Oh, Max!' until I was crying, too, though I never realized it till afterwards, when I found my cheeks all wet. Needless to say, by this time the old boys in the other two beds were beginning to stir. One of them opened his eyes and just lay there, gaping. The other reached out for his teeth, which were on the bedside table. And all of a sudden, as if the emotion were more than a dog could bear, Max pointed his nose into the air and began on this long-drawn-out, melancholy howling, which is absolutely the most heart-rending sound in the world.

That is when it all broke up. I suppose one of the patients in another cubicle must have alerted the nursing staff, or maybe the noise of Max's barking had penetrated to the far end of the ward. Of course it was bound to happen. I'd known all along that we would be discovered. It was too much to hope that you could smuggle a dog both in *and* out of a hospital ward without anyone raising the alarm. The nurse who came running was one of the senior ones, she wore a blue belt with a silver buckle and had this frilly cap and arm bands. She was blazing with rage. I've never seen anyone in such a stew. She said, 'GET THAT DOG OUT OF HERE!' as if Max was something obnoxious. Maybe to her he was. But he wasn't to David, and that was what mattered.

'How *dare* you bring that animal into the wards? And to put him on a patient's *bed*! Don't you know this boy has had a leg amputated?' (The cow. She didn't have to *say* it.) 'Do you realize the damage you could have done? Do you realize the *germs* you have spread? Do you have the least idea—'

'I'm sorry,' I said. But I wasn't; I wasn't in the least bit sorry. David had been reunited with Max, and that was all I cared.

The worst part was *dis*uniting them. I felt dreadful, prising Max away. He clung, with his front paws, and David had tears streaming down his face, and it was like one of those awful B movies where little kids are torn screaming from the arms of their loving foster parents to be forcibly handed over to people who you know (because it's that sort of film) are going to batter them nigh unto death. I had to remind myself that nobody was going to batter Max and that in another week or two David would be back home anyway. But I do think hospitals are the most brutish institutions. They might be great on cutting people's legs off and pumping them full of drugs, but they're lousy, if you ask me, on human emotions.

Max wouldn't walk when I finally managed to get him away from David. He just dug in his feet and put his head down and refused to budge. I wasn't going to drag him; not with David looking on. I knew he couldn't bear to see him dragged. So I picked him up, and moved off, across the shouting virago, with what dignity I could muster (which wasn't very much, with Max struggling and kicking in his attempts to break free) and at the corner of the cubicle I turned and said: 'It was worth it, wasn't it?' and David managed a nod and a bit of a grin before the virago got at him and started yanking and pummelling and rending at the bedclothes in her frenzy, presumably, to dislodge all the germs.

Outside, I met up with Zoot. He looked critically at my face and said, 'How'd it go?'

'Got turned out,' I said.

'Were they mad?'

'Like a hornet.'

Zoot looked glum.

'There'll be trouble,' he said.

I turned on him.

'I don't care! Do you hear me? I don't care! I did what I came to do, and I'm glad!'

The journey back was long and tedious, and, inevitably, an anti-climax. We had to wait thirty minutes for the bus, and as Max still wouldn't walk, and as I refused to pull him and Zoot refused to carry him, we all just stayed where we were in the bus station, drinking in the diesel fumes and eating stale sandwiches that tasted like feet.

Zoot actually was pretty good. He came all the way back out to the farm with me, even though it meant a double bus ride for him. We let Max off the lead at the bottom of the lane and he went trotting off into the yard of his own accord, so at least we didn't have to run the gauntlet through to the paddock a second time. Zoot was a bit anxious in case someone might have noticed he was missing, but I said that country dogs weren't like town dogs: Max quite often went off exploring by himself.

It was five o'clock when I got home. I felt that it should have been later—I felt I'd been out all the day and half the night. Mumps said, 'You look tired! What have you been up to?' And then, peering at my sweater: 'You're covered in hairs!'

'Been talking to a dog,' I said.

I knew it was quite possible that later that night, after David's parents had been to visit him, there would be an angry telephone call. I knew that if Pop were to learn what had happened he would be furious with me. He would say that as a doctor's daughter I ought to know better. He would be ashamed lest someone at the hospital find out who I was.

'Dr Mather's daughter . . . taking a *dog* in!'

I knew all that, but I still didn't care—and the telephone call still didn't come. I thought that maybe David's parents, being accustomed to have animals about the place, might not see my crime in quite so heinous a light as the robots that ran the hospital. At least, that was what I hoped.

At half past nine the telephone *did* ring, but it was Zoot, to say he'd just had this ghastly thought . . .

109

'Suppose someone tells your old man? He'll do his nut!' I said yes, he probably would, but with me, not with Zoot. Zoot said, 'Well, but I was as much to blame. I didn't have to let myself get roped in.' It was noble of him, but I wouldn't have shopped him; not unless I really had to.

(In fact, I never did. News did eventually get back to Pop but not till ages later; by which time, he said, he hadn't the heart to give me the telling off that I deserved.)

I went to bed shortly after Zoot's phone call feeling both emotionally and physically exhausted, but still defiant. Even when I woke up in the night and remembered David crying—*David*, who I had never known to show any signs of weakness—I still felt that what I had done was justified. After all, even crying was better than showing no feelings at all. At least if he cried it meant that he *cared*; and as long as he cared, then that meant he had a reason for living.

7

I was sure that Abbey would say something next morning. She was in the common room when I arrived, sorting out books in her locker. I said, 'Hi!' and braced myself. Abbey said: 'I've got another rounders practice arranged for twelve-thirty. I hope you're going to do better than you did last time?'

After recovering myself, I said, 'I had things on my mind last time.' To wit, finding some way of restoring David's spirits. 'Have you—ah—decided to play, after all?'

'Yes. I thought about it,' said Abbey, 'and I realized that you were quite right. One can't just stop doing things because—well.' She yanked a book out of her locker. 'Things *do* have to go on.'

It seemed that that was all she was going to say. I waited for something else, but she just clapped a pile of books together, closed up her locker and said, 'Twelve-thirty, OK?'

'Yes,' I said. 'OK.' The bell rang for assembly. I followed Abbey across to the door. 'Did you—see David last night?'

'Mm.'

'How was he?'

There was a pause.

'He wants to go home,' said Abbey.

'*Does* he?' I said. I must have said it somewhat over-enthusiastically, because she turned, with raised eyebrows, to look at me. 'That's *good*,' I said. 'It shows he's starting to take an interest again. It's got to be an improvement!' Abbey didn't say anything. 'Well, hasn't it?' I said.

111

Of course it had! It stood to reason. Last week he hadn't cared about anything at all: this week he wanted to go home. Wanted to start living again. And all because of Max—because of me.

Abbey obviously didn't know; David couldn't have told her. I toyed, during assembly, with the idea of giving her the full run-down, but before I had the chance I found myself nobbled by Willie.

'Robyn!' She crooked a finger as we filed from the hall. 'Could I have a word with you?'

I'd been expecting the *Windbag* to get stuck in—'And where, pray, were you, miss, yesterday afternoon? If you really consider yourself above the need to benefit from my teaching', etc. etc.—but I hadn't been expecting Willie. After all, what was it to do with her?

'Let's find somewhere quiet,' she said. She opened a door and peered in, her old pea-head nid-nodding on the end of its stem-like neck. 'The Library! This will do. Come and sit down.'

She pulled out a chair at one of the tables. Somewhat mutinously, I seated myself opposite to her.

'I understand,' she said, 'that you and Tom Kearns' (she meant Zoot: I always had to shake myself to realize that Tom was his proper name) 'absented yourselves from school yesterday afternoon?'

It wasn't any *business* of hers.

'I gather you went to the hospital, to see David?'

'Yes,' I said.

'I also gather that you'—that we what?—'introduced a bit of canine havoc into the place?'

I looked at her, cautiously. Did Willie have an unsuspected sense of humour?

'We took his dog in,' I said. '*I* took it in. It wasn't Z—Tom's fault. I bullied him.'

'Yes, I can imagine,' said Willie.

She could imagine! *What* could she imagine? She'd better not try having a go at me; not the mood I was in. I'd done what had to be done and I was glad of it. What did that withered old prune know about anything? About dogs, or David, or being young, or—

'I hardly need to tell you,' said Willie, 'that it was a highly irresponsible action coming from a person of your years—and of your background! If anyone should have known better, it's you.'

I flared up at that. (I don't know whether it's true about people with red hair having quick tempers, but I certainly do have a very low flashpoint. So does Pop, who's also reddish.)

'I did it for a reason! It wasn't just something silly—it wasn't just a joke!'

'No, I never thought that it was.'

'I did it to help him!'

'In what way, exactly,' said Willie, 'did you think that it would help?'

'I thought it would take him out of himself —take his mind off things. And it did! It did him good! He *enjoyed* having Max there!'

'He did, maybe, at the time,' said Willie. (*May*be? I was with him, I saw him, I *knew*.) 'You weren't there afterwards, were you? And neither was I, you're quite right! So what does the desiccated old bat know about anything, anyway?'

I blinked.

'All I can tell you,' said Willie, 'is what his mother told me. No!' She held up a hand, silencing another outburst. 'She hasn't been complaining—you're lucky. David happens to have a very understanding mother. She just asked me to speak to you and to try and explain how it is that although you meant well, it

113

wasn't actually, in the circumstances, the right thing to do.'

I opened my mouth, in automatic protest. 'But he—'

'He was overjoyed at the time, I don't doubt. But it's not just at the time one has to think about: it's later. When you've gone off, and you've taken the dog with you, and David's left by himself . . . did you ever stop to consider how he might feel then?'

I frowned, and was silent. What was she driving at?

'I don't have to tell you,' said Willie, 'that David is very ill. He knows that he's very ill, and the only way he can cope with it, even just the idea of it, is to cut himself off—shut himself away. Wounded animals do it: so do wounded human beings. They don't have dens to hide in, so what they do is what David's done, put up barriers, emotional blocks to protect themselves. What you did, with the best of intentions, was to tear it all down. But it was like tearing away living tissue, and when you tear tissue it bleeds, it leaves a raw wound. And that was the state you left David in. You brought it all back to him—all the things he's been protecting himself against. The things he's missing. The things he's scared he might never have again. His dog, for example. I believe his dog means a lot to him?'

'Everything!' I said. 'That's why—'

'I know: that's why you did it. You thought that if David could only be with his dog, even just for a few minutes, it would work wonders, psychologically —force him to think about the dog rather than about himself. Which it did; undoubtedly. Your reasoning was perfectly sound, it's just the timing that was out.'

I looked at her, scowling. I wasn't scowling because

I was mad, but because I was remembering David crying, and beginning, reluctantly, to cotton on to what she was trying to tell me. Willie obviously misinterpreted. She sighed, and dibbled with a fingertip in her old grey bird's nest of hair, shifting the hairpins about.

'I'm probably not being fair . . . it's probably something you can't be expected to understand unless you've ever been ill. Really ill. Which I don't expect you have?'

I shook my head. I couldn't ever remember being ill at all, not even chicken-pox or mumps. The monthly gripes was the only thing I'd ever had to endure. (I felt ashamed, now, of all the fuss I used to make: it was such a little thing to suffer, compared with what David was going through.)

'I was really ill once,' said Willie. 'Years ago, when I was young. Not as young as David—in fact, you probably wouldn't think it was young at all, but I did. I was thirty-two. It didn't seem to me any sort of age at which to die. But even apart from the possibility of dying . . . do you know the very worst thing about it?'

Again, I shook my head. I wondered if Willie talked to Abbey like this (and if so, whether Abbey found it as embarrassing as I did: I had never wanted revelations from Willie).

'The worst thing,' said Willie, 'was thinking about my little cat. Sometimes, you know, we unmarried folk can become extraordinarily attached to our animals. My little cat meant all the world to me—and I'd had to abandon her to strangers. It broke my heart to lie there, wondering how she was, and whether I should ever see her again.'

'Did you?' I said.

'Oh, yes! She was there waiting for me when I came

115

out, all sleek and complacent and *very* well fed. She hadn't suffered—but I had! At the time I missed her so much it tore me to pieces just thinking about her. And like David, I couldn't afford the luxury of being torn to pieces. I needed all the strength I could spare for myself. So I had quite consciously to close my mind to the little cat and say, I won't think about her, I'll just think about me . . . and that's what David's been doing. And what he has to do. What *you* have to do—you and Tom and Abbey—is to try to understand and be patient. Not feel hurt at being excluded, not think that he's given up just because he seems withdrawn. If he's self-absorbed it's because that's what's necessary for survival. He'll come back to you when he's ready; when he feels strong enough. But he has to be allowed to do it at his own pace. Just bear with him. That's the best support you can give him at the moment.'

I didn't go to visit David in hospital again. Apart from the fact that they almost certainly wouldn't have let me in, I was even less sure than before that he would want me there. Zoot went once, rather nervously, but caught sight of David's brother and instantly fled in a panic. (It's funny about Zoot: for all his big talk of how he was going to travel the world and have adventures—of how he was going to row the Atlantic single-handed, cross the Sahara on a bicycle, ski his way down the Amazon, all or any of which things he might by now very well have done—when it came to personal confrontations he definitely lacked what I would call resolution. What he himself would call *bottle*. I remember I accused him of it after the Ned incident, and he got quite heated. He said, 'All right, big mouth! You go!' But it was different for me. I was the one who'd actually done the deed: it was me they'd be gunning for. And anyway, *I*'d never boasted of how I was going to shoot the rapids of the Nile in a soap dish.)

We had to rely on Abbey for the latest bulletins. At first they continued glum, so that I didn't like asking, but then after a bit, to my immense relief—because Willie's lecture had really rattled me—they started to perk up and get a bit more positive. First she told us they had fitted him with an artificial leg (she was so happy about it, I didn't like to correct her and say that it wasn't an artificial leg but only a temporary prosthesis and that they would fit a proper one later on. It sounded too know-it-all and nitpicking), then she told us that he was starting to walk, then that he *could* walk, but with sticks, then with only one stick, and then, at last, that they were letting him come home.

I remember the day she told us that. It was the week of half-term and she was all flushed and excited. She'd been to see Mr Francis and he'd said she could stay off school that day so she could meet up with David's mother and go back with her and David to the farm. I hadn't seen Abbey so buoyant in a long time. I'd grown so used, these last few weeks, to her being down that I'd almost forgotten what the real Abbey was like. Zoot and I agreed that we'd give anything to have her bullying and bossing us again, taking charge of our consciences, organizing us into doing what we knew to be right but were too morally flimsy to do for ourselves. I even solemnly vowed, in front of Zoot, that if God made David better I would attend every single CND meeting and go on every single march and demo that Abbey wanted me to go on for the whole of the next school year.

Next day, I remember Abbey coming up to me and

saying, 'Robyn, you are such a goon! How *could* you?'
She said that David had finally told her about me
smuggling Max in and the terrible scene that had
ensued. He had kept them in stitches, she said, re-
enacting it at the dinner table. It made me feel better,
hearing that—the fact that David could laugh about it.
Abbey said I wouldn't have laughed if I had been there
that night, at the hospital, and had seen the state he
was in.

'He said he didn't care what happened to him, he
didn't want any more treatment, he just wanted to
come home.'

'Well, but now he is home,' I said, 'so it's all OK,
isn't it?'

'It is *now*,' said Abbey. 'It wasn't then.'

'Oh, Abbey, don't dwell!' I said. She is a terrible girl
for dwelling. 'Sufficient unto the day, or whatever it is
. . . Shakespeare?'

Abbey looked at me.

'Shakespeare!' she said. 'It's the *Bible*.'

On the Thursday of that week it was Guild Day—the
day before half-term, when we bedecked various parts
of the school in finery and organized events for
charity. The first years were acting a play they had
written, the second had an indoor bazaar going in the
assembly hall, there was an art display in the gym,
morris dancing on the front lawn, aquabatics in the
swimming pool. There was also, of course, Abbey's
sponsored rounders.

We spent most of the day setting up. I kept remembering how last year, when we'd been in the fifth,
we'd decorated the classroom to look like a puppet
booth and had all dressed up as different
figures—Zoot and I had been Punch and Judy, Pilch

118

had been the Policeman, Little Jane had been dog Toby. David and Abbey had been more romantic: they had been Harlequin and Columbine . . . someone's elderly aunt had been so smitten that she'd got out her camera and taken a snap. She had sent them a copy afterwards and it had appeared in the school magazine.

At twelve o'clock we all queued up for packed lunches from the tea tent (in charge of the Home Ecs department) and at one o'clock the parents and other guests began to arrive. In thirty minutes our rounders match was due to begin. I suggested to Abbey that we went off to get changed and collect up the bats and everything, but she seemed agitated at the idea and said, 'Not yet, there's no rush, we don't have to go yet.' It was unlike Abbey, because as a rule she's most tremendously keen on having everything all ready and waiting hours beforehand. Now all she wanted to do was hang around the car park and watch the visitors arrive. I understood the reason a few minutes later when Zoot came charging up and panted, 'David's here!' Abbey's face went bright scarlet. (She told me afterwards that he had said he might come along, but she'd been trying not to build her hopes too high in case at the last minute he'd decided he couldn't face it.) Zoot said that he'd just seen the car turn into the car park—'the Church Road entrance'. Abbey was off before he had even finished speaking. As she rounded the corner by the bicycle sheds she paused, briefly, to look back at us.

'Aren't you coming?'

'Do you want us to?'

'Yes, come on!'

Abbey went plunging off again, leaving Zoot and me to follow. We trailed, rather. I pretended to myself that what we were doing was being tactful, giving Abbey a chance to greet David on her own, without our grinning, intrusive presences, but of course it wasn't that at all. The truth was that I was feeling apprehensive, and I suspect that Zoot was, too. I think that he, like me, was uncertain what to say, what attitude to adopt. How *do* you greet one of your oldest and closest friends when they've been through what David had?

David solved the problem for us. He had Max with him, and the minute he saw us he snatched him up and shouted, 'Watch it! Dognappers!' which immediately broke the ice. I did glance rather warily at Ned (he had taken time off work to bring David in) but all he said, as he pocketed the car keys, was, 'Yes . . . that's a scene I should like to have witnessed!'

We took them over to the playing field, to watch the rounders. David was walking quite well, though he still had to use a stick and of course he couldn't bend his leg (he would be able to later when they gave him his proper one) which made the slope leading up from the car park a bit difficult, but Zoot and I, when we talked about it afterwards, both reckoned it was pretty good going. After all, he'd only been up and about for a short while; and as Zoot said, he was walking better *now* than he had been *before*. (I felt really incensed, later that afternoon, when Little Jane came up to me in tears in the cloakroom and gulped, 'Oh, Robyn! It's so dreadful!' I said, 'What's so dreadful?' and she said, 'Seeing David like that!' I could have hit her. I had to remind myself that *she* hadn't seen him as I had seen him, the day I'd smuggled Max in.)

The rounders match went really well. The final score was Us fifteen, Them (pardon me while I cough) thirty-six. We raised £52 for charity, Pilch whammed no less than six balls over the tennis courts, Zoot managed to break a bat and Max ran on to the pitch and scarpered with one of the posts.

Max running on to the pitch was in some ways the highlight of the game: it certainly got the biggest round of applause. It was David, in the end (after a lot of running and shouting, and Ned in the middle of it trying to exercise some kind of non-existent authority), who had to go out there and do a retrieving act for us. A great cheer went up as he came back. It was the sort of half-mocking but good-natured cheer that audiences give when something has gone wrong and has now been put right; but more than that, it was a personal cheer for David. He acknowledged it, solemnly taking a bow, then raising the post above his head like a weight lifter lifting his weights. I was glad he hadn't lost his sense of humour.

Afterwards we left Ned and David in the tea tent while we went off to change. It was while we were changing that Little Jane infuriated me by her stupid blubbing—just as I'd been feeling so happy and thinking how *good* David looked. Why do people have to be so crass?—and Abbey told me how she'd been hoping that David would come but hadn't been counting on it, which was why she hadn't said anything to Zoot and me, in case at the last moment his nerve had failed him. He was going off tomorrow morning, she said, to stay with his grandmother in Wales for a fortnight. After that he was coming back to school. Today was like a sort of ice-breaker.

I could see that it must be an ordeal for him, having to come back and face everyone—knowing that they knew and were all going to be looking at him. All going to be *speculating*. I was glad, at any rate, that he'd missed out on the blubbing.

When we went back outside we discovered Ned and David, together with Zoot, chucking hooplas at Sophie's hoopla stall in the bazaar. Sophie, all pink and beaming, had eyes for no one but David. She spared Abbey and me just one quick, resentful glance.

'You might have *told* me,' she said.

'Told you what?' said Abbey.

Zoot threw a hoopla, neatly encircling a box of matches.

'Told her that God was going to be here.'

'You might have said,' said Sophie. She was plainly feeling aggrieved: things were being kept from her again.

'I didn't know, either,' I said.

'Neither did God,' said David. 'God wasn't at all sure that he mightn't get a cold foot.'

Sophie looked up at him, puzzled. (I did hope that we weren't going to start on the foot jokes again; I really didn't think they were terribly funny. Neither did Abbey, I could tell.)

'Tenderfoot, barefoot, cold *feet*. Cold feet is very footist. I'm thinking of starting a—'

'Hey!' yelled Zoot. 'I've been swindled!' He had opened his matchbox to find that instead of matches it contained a ring (one of the cheap, make-it-yourself sort, where you choose your own stone and stick it on with special glue). 'Where's my matches?'

'It's not matches.' Sophie pointed coldly to a large handwritten notice which said HOOPLA SURPRISE! WIN A BOX AND SEE WHAT'S IN IT.

'Aha!' said Zoot. 'Just as well I didn't try for that packet of Durex.'

'What packet of Jurex?' said Sophie. (There wasn't one, of course; not in a second-year bazaar.) 'What's Jurex, anyway?'

'Never you mind,' said Abbey. (Absolutely *no* grasp of child psychology.)

'Go and ask your little friends,' said Zoot.

'I'm asking you!' said Sophie. She turned, trustingly, to David. 'What's—'

'Who wants an engagement ring? No-carat, junk jewellery, guaranteed drop to pieces within the week . . . who wants to get engaged? You want to get engaged?' Zoot seized David's hand. 'There you go! Perfect fit! How's about that?'

'Ooh, lovely!' said David. 'Give us a kiss!'

They all moved on, leaving me behind to solace Sophie. She was obviously feeling hard-done-by. She wanted to know about Jurex, and what David had meant by cold feet being footist. I found the second even harder to explain than the first. I suddenly realized that nobody had ever actually told Sophie the truth: as far as she was concerned, David had just gone into hospital for an operation on his leg and the reason he had to walk funny and use a stick was that he was still in plaster. It shook me, rather. I had taken it for granted that everybody knew, but of course only the sixth had been talked to by Mr Francis. I somehow managed to fudge it, but I could tell she was growing suspicious.

'David is all right now,' she said, 'isn't he?'

'Well, you can see,' I said.

Sophie stared frowningly up the hall, to where David and the rest were grouped round a stall selling what looked like hand-knitted caterpillars. (It turned out they were draught excluders for doors.)

'He won't have to go into hospital again, will he?'

What was I supposed to say? Desperately I tried to think back to what Pop had told me. All I could remember was that the beastly hateful drugs would

123

have to be continued for at least two years; but as to whether he would have to go back into hospital—

'*Will* he?' said Sophie.

'Well, just like for outpatients and things,' I said. 'Maybe the odd day or two . . . hey, look! You've got customers. You'd better go see to them or you'll lose business.'

When I caught up with the others I found that Pilch had joined them. I thought that was quite brave of him, actually. Most people were either too embarrassed or too shy. I heard Pilch saying, '. . . yours if you want it!' and David's reply, 'All those lines? You must be joking!' and I knew that Pilch had been offering him his part back again.

'I'll tell you what,' said David. 'Next term we'll do *Treasure Island* and I can play Silver . . . I've even got the parrot!' He scooped up Max and set him on his shoulder. 'Pieces of eight, pieces of eight!'

I could see that the others weren't going to respond as they should. Pilch was looking uncomfortable, Zoot was looking at his shoes, Abbey wearing what I call her any-minute-now expression. Even Ned had transferred his gaze to the middle distance. It was clearly a case of Robyn to the rescue. I leapt in: 'Hey, that's not fair! What do I get to play?'

'You can play Blind Spew . . . aaargh!' David pretended to hawk: it was an old joke.

'Pew, you idiot! And anyway, *some part*. What about Ben Gunn?'

'Oh, that's Zoot! Zoot to a tee!'

'Thanks very much,' said Zoot.

We left the bazaar and wandered back into the grounds. David and Abbey walked a bit ahead, hand-holding like the old days. The rest of us—me and Ned and Zoot: Pilch had peeled off—idled purposefully, keeping our distance.

Zoot wanted to know from Ned how long it would be before David could start playing cricket. Ned said, 'Not this term.'

'Next term?' I said. (I was only trying to be helpful.)

Zoot looked at me witheringly.

'Next term's football!'

'Yes, I'm afraid there isn't any chance of that,' said Ned. 'He won't ever be able to run properly again, you know.'

'Oh,' said Zoot, and his face fell: he obviously hadn't realized.

I noticed, as we walked, that several members of staff came up to say hallo to David, including Willie and the Windbag. (Not together. It was a known fact that they loathed each other—which I am inclined to believe is a point in Willie's favour rather than the Windbag's.) I asked Abbey afterwards what they'd said, but she just looked vague and said, 'Oh, the usual things.' She added that Willie had been a couple of times to visit David in hospital, which was something I hadn't known. I wondered if he had enjoyed being visited by Willie, and what they had found to talk about.

At four o'clock we gathered for tea and sandwiches in the tea tent. Ned said that after tea he thought it would probably be time for him and David to start making tracks. I asked whether David mightn't stay on. I said that we'd arranged to take our supper down on to the beach and then go on to Uncle Jax for an hour or two. (Uncle Jax was a disco which had recently opened up. Being in Clearhaven it was about as raving as a church youth club: if you really wanted a wild time, you went over to Brighton. I couldn't see that there could be any possible objection to

David coming to Uncle Jax.)

'We'd take care of him,' I said.

Ned smiled and said yes, he was sure that we would, but the fact was they had to be up at the crack of dawn tomorrow for the drive to Wales and David needed a full night's rest.

'Doctor's orders,' he said; and then, as an after-thought: 'Your father's, probably! Daren't argue with that.'

I supposed not, though I thought it was a shame. I thought David would have enjoyed coming to Jax with us.

We went down to the beach later, as planned. Pilch and Andy came, and the two Janes. We did a bit of swimming and a bit of lying around, exchanged a bit of gossip, had a bit of a laugh. I told them about Sophie and the Jurex, and Pilch said, 'What is the world coming to? In our day every self-respecting second-year knew what Durex was!'

Zoot then told a joke about a Scotsman, which produced hoots from Pilch and Andy, giggles from me and Big Jane, shriek from Little Jane. Abbey then says: 'I think that joke was racist.'

Groans. Pilch says, 'If you think *that* one's racist—' and proceeds to tell this really awful corny one about an Irishman, a Welshman and a Jew. After that, we had a whole succession of jokes. Andy told one about a fairy who sat on a toadstool (Little Jane had to have it explained to her) and I started to tell one and then forgot the punch line, which is what I usually do with jokes. We didn't talk about David at all, even though he was obviously on everybody's mind. No one even mentioned him until we'd been up to the hot dog stall and were eating hot dogs, sitting on the breakwater, dipping our toes in the sea, when Big Jane said: 'Why

126

didn't David come?' I explained (because Abbey always went silent when anyone talked about David) that they were off to Wales next morning and had to be up early. Little Jane said: 'In any case, it wouldn't be much fun for him, would it?'

'What wouldn't?' I said.

'Well—' She suddenly went all confused and bashful. 'Not being able to swim or anything.'

'He can swim!' I said. To be perfectly honest I didn't know whether he could, yet, but I knew that he *would* be able to. It maddened me when people assumed that he was going to be some kind of a cripple. 'He could even go water skiing,' I said, 'if he wanted.'

Big Jane leaned forward, peering round Pilch in order to look at me.

'*Really?*' she said.

'Yes, really!' I said.

'I knew this guy once,' said Andy, 'just used to take his leg off and jump in . . . he was about sixty. Bloody incredible!'

'Why did he have to take his leg off?' Big Jane wanted to know.

'Oh, for goodness' sake!' I said.

Big Jane looked hurt. 'Well, *I* don't know,' she said, 'do I?'

Little Jane said, 'I don't think I should like to do that.'

I turned on her. I was beginning to feel rather aggressive.

'Wouldn't like to do what?'

'Take my leg off.'

'Why not?'

She squirmed.

'I'd feel people were staring at me.'

'So let them!'

'Easier said than done,' said Pilch.

I tossed my head.

'I wouldn't care!'

It was a lie, of course; of course I would care. In many ways, I'm quite rampantly vain. I think what I was really saying was that they had just better get used to the idea and not try staring at David. I *think* that's what I was saying.

'Let's go to Jax!'

Zoot all this time had been sitting as silent as Abbey. Now he suddenly plunged off the breakwater and began forging back, with long overarm strokes, towards the beach. There wasn't any need for him to swim so vigorously, the tide was coming in fast, it would have carried him there quite easily. I guess it was just Zoot's way of expressing his feelings.

As we were getting dressed (we'd left our clothes in a heap, beneath the sea wall) Abbey said, 'You lot go on to Jax. I'm not sure that I feel like it.'

'Abbey!' I said. 'You must!'

'She doesn't have to,' said Zoot.

I watched as Abbey moved away from us, over the pebbles, towards the slope that led up to the promenade.

'She's going to do a broody,' I said.

'So maybe she needs to.'

'But it's not good for her!'

'How do you know?' said Zoot.

There was a silence. Abbey reached the top of the slope, turned, waved, and disappeared. Little Jane made a hiccuping sound.

'Poor Abbey! It must be so ghastly for her!'

If she starts yipping, I thought, I shall scream.

She didn't yip. We went on to Jax, where we stayed till almost midnight, and I danced a bit with Zoot and quite a lot with Pilch and a couple of times with Andy, and afterwards Pilch took me home in his mother's car, which he had borrowed for the evening—he lived out our way so it was no problem for him—but Andy was there, in the back, so there wasn't any funny business.

My parents were still up when I got in. I said that we'd been to Jax and that I'd wanted David to come but Ned had said no.

'Quite right,' said Pop. He said I had to remember that David wasn't up to full strength yet. 'He's only just come out of hospital . . . give the lad a chance!'

Mumps said she thought it was 'ever so plucky of him, going out there on the rounders field like that.'

'If he hadn't,' I said, 'we'd never have got the post back. David's the only one Max takes any notice of. That day—'

I stopped. 'That day I smuggled him into hospital' was what I had been going to say. Fortunately for me, at that point, Pop started in on a dissertation about people adapting to disabilities, and how young people adapted better than older ones, and the subject of Max was forgotten.

Next morning Abbey rang me. She asked me if we'd had a good time last night and she said that she'd spoken with David on the telephone and had then had a bath and gone to bed. And then she said, 'I think I've found a way of coping . . . I think you just have to take each day as it comes.'

'Well, yes,' I said. 'I don't see that there's much else one *can* do, what with the Bomb and everything.'

'This is it,' said Abbey.

She really sounded as if she'd worked out a whole new philosophy of life.

8

We were discussing what we could do to mark David's homecoming. We all felt it was an occasion, and that as such it should not be allowed to pass unnoticed.

'What we need,' I said, 'is a sort of welcome-back ceremony.'

'A party,' said Zoot.

We looked at Abbey, seeking approval.

'Party?' I said.

'Mm . . .' She considered the idea. 'You mean, just us? or—'

'Just our year,' said Zoot.

'But that's over fifty people!'

'Just *some* of our year.'

'Which ones?'

We made out a list there and then: Pilch, Andy, the two Janes; the *whole* of the cricket Eleven; Avril Ellison—

'Avril *Elli*son?'

'She always gets left out of things,' said Abbey.

'Look, this is a party,' I said. 'For *David*. Not a lonely hearts club. If she's going to come we might just as well invite the lot and be done with it.'

'Not Whinge,' said Zoot.

We agreed not Whinge: Whinge was insufferable. We finally got it down to twenty, which meant there was only one place to have it and that was mine. Zoot's was too small and too crowded; and Abbey's mum, although hospitable, always grew nervous about 'crowds of young folk'. She thought crowds (a crowd to her was more than three) meant drink and drugs

130

and the smashing up of furniture.

'And anyway, there's Sophie.'

It seemed at this time that Abbey was going through a bad patch with Sophie, or perhaps they were going through a bad patch with each other. Abbey was certainly far less tolerant than she usually was, and Sophie, probably, more trying. I knew she felt left out and badly treated. I had asked Abbey, after Guild Day, whether she didn't think that Sophie ought to have things explained to her, but all she had said was, 'Why?' And then, before I could answer, 'She'd only get all possessive and start trying to take over.' It struck me as such a funny thing to say.

Anyway, I promised that I would put the idea of a party to my parents and see how they reacted. I didn't anticipate any problems, they've always been pretty good about things like that. Mumps used to say that since they'd 'failed in their duty' to provide me with a brother or sister the least they could do was let me invite my friends back whenever I wanted. When I asked her about the party, she said, 'I haven't any objection.'

I looked across at Pop. He shrugged his shoulders, fatalistically.

'So is that OK, then?'

'You'd better just check with David's mother first,' said Mumps.

Check with David's mother? Why should I need to check with David's mother? David was seventeen! He didn't have to consult his *mother*.

'Just to be on the safe side. After all, you wouldn't want to go arranging a big welcome home and then find yourself left with egg on your face, would you? For all you know, his family might have something of their own lined up.'

131

'Oh.' I hadn't thought of that. 'OK, so if I check with her and she says they haven't, we can go ahead?'

'Yes, but I shouldn't invite too many people if I were you; I should try to limit it to no more than about a dozen. Don't forget he's not going to be absolutely one hundred per cent yet.'

I didn't tell her we'd finally settled for twenty. I thought, however, that I would try to talk Zoot into dropping some of the cricket team. I didn't really see that David would *want* all the cricket team to be there, carrying on about their silly little batting averages and the number of wickets they'd taken. I thought that if I were David I should be impatient to get going on all the new things I could tackle (such as water skiing and mountain climbing) rather than dwelling on the old ones that I couldn't. I decided, in fact, that the cricket team would be tactless, and I made up my mind to tell Zoot so.

I also made up my mind, that same evening, to cycle out to the farm. Mumps said, 'Why not just give them a call?' but Mumps didn't know my guilty secret regarding Max. I still felt a bit bad about that. Even though everything was all right *now*, it hadn't, as Abbey said, been all right at the time. I thought that the least I could do was see his mother and explain myself.

It was half past eight when I cycled into the yard. David's parents were sitting in the kitchen at the old, scrubbed, wooden table, finishing their supper. The back door was open and the geese were wandering about, slap-slapping across the flagstones on their big plappy feet. The goat, just able to reach on the end of its tether, was standing with its head inside the doorway. Max was sitting bolt upright on a chair (David's, I suspected) and three cats were hunched together in a

132

watchful row upon the dresser. Ned wasn't there: he has his own flat up in town and only comes home, as a rule, at weekends. I could have wished that David's father wasn't there, too. Not that he hasn't always been perfectly pleasant, in a casual sort of way, it's just that he bears this quite incredible resemblance to David, which I find disconcerting.

The first thing I noticed (I have trained myself to notice these things, I think that as an actress one should) was that they both looked what Zoot would call absolutely shagged. David's mother was leaning forward with her elbows on the table, the tips of her fingers pressed against her eyelids. His father was slumped back in his chair, with his feet propped up on the edge of the dresser. I reminded myself that these were working farmers who probably rose with the dawn, so when Mrs Geary offered me a coffee I said thank you, but I'd just had supper. I said I'd only come to ask them a very quick question and then I'd be off. She said, 'That sounds intriguing! At least take a seat—push Max out of the way. Max, get down! You shouldn't be sitting at table, anyway.'

She only said that for show. I knew he sat there all the time, because David had told us. Another thing he'd told us was that quite often the cats marauded about the table helping themselves to whatever took their fancy, and that when visitors came his mother would snatch them up and throw them on the floor, pretending to be horrified, as if they'd never done such a thing in their lives before. I guess that was why nobody had made such a big production about me smuggling Max into the hospital. It was, of course, my cue for doing my explanation bit, but somehow, with David's father there, and me knowing him even less than I knew Mrs Geary, I lost my nerve; that plus the fact that I'd promised to ask just the one question and then go.

'Have a potato.' David's mother pushed a dish towards me. 'Or would you rather have some strawberries? Just help yourself, they're all going begging.' She sat back, hoisting Max on to her lap. 'So what is it, that you wanted to ask?'

'Well,' I said, 'it's about David. What we w—'

Mr Geary suddenly swung his feet down from the dresser.

'Forgive me! Just remembered something.'

As he went through the door, the cats streaked after him. Max streaked after the cats, the geese splatted after Max, even the goat withdrew its head. Mrs Geary and I were left alone. There was a pause.

'About David,' said Mrs Geary.

'Yes.' Since they were on offer, I pulled the dish of potatoes towards me. (Contrary to myth, potatoes are *not* fattening.) 'What we're doing, we're trying to organize this party for him. A sort of'—they must have been fresh dug from the fields, those potatoes. They tasted all earthy and sweet—'a sort of welcome-home. We wondered, if we arranged it for Saturday week, would that be all right?'

'I see no reason why not.'

'It's just we thought perhaps you might have something else planned.'

'No,' she said, 'we've nothing else. We had our little celebration when he came out of hospital.'

'Oh, great! I'll tell Abbey to tell him, then.'

'How *is* Abbey?' said Mrs Geary.

I hesitated, not quite sure how she meant it. Did she mean, 'How is Abbey' like in 'Hallo, good morning, how are you?' Or did she mean—

'I mean . . . how do *you* think she is? You see more

134

of her than we do. You're closest to her. Is she managing, do you think? Really?'

I thought, really, that Abbey was the sort who would always manage, one way or another. She might crumble a bit at the edges, but she would never go totally to pieces. On the other hand, that wasn't to say she couldn't suffer just as much anguish as the next person.

'It bothers me,' said Mrs Geary. 'She's such a good girl. She's been so brave. So . . . mature. I've been able to talk to Abbey almost more than I've been able to talk to—well! To anyone, almost. But I do worry about her. I worry about what it's doing to her. I sometimes think we should never have let her and David become so close, but—oh! I don't know. At the time . . . what can one do?'

She was asking *me*? Alarmed, I pulled the strawberries towards me. I hadn't come here for this. I'd just come to arrange for the party.

'The thing about Abbey,' I said, stuffing strawberries into my mouth, 'the thing about Abbey is that she works things out. She goes away and broods, and then she comes up to you and says, I've found a way of coping: I've found a way of dealing with it. With—you know—whatever the problem is.'

'I know; she's a sensible girl. A very sensible girl. But so young! You're all of you . . . so young!'

I concentrated my attention on the strawberries.

'About this party,' I mumbled.

'Yes. Yes, tell me about it! Where is it going to be?'

'We're going to have it at my place. I've asked my parents and they say it's OK. We thought what we'd do, we'd make this cake—well, Abbey'll make it, because if I made it it'd turn out like a lump of granite—and we'll think up something to put on it, like welcome home or something, only, you know, nothing that yukkish. I expect what'll happen, Zoot'll make up a joke, one of his really corny ones, and everyone'll die groaning. But anyway, what we thought—'

'Robyn!' Mrs Geary suddenly leaned forward, rather urgently, across the table. 'You won't expect too much of him, will you? Of David, I mean. You won't—'

'We won't make him tired,' I said. I wanted to show her that we weren't irresponsible (despite being so young). 'We're only going to invite just a few people; just from our year. And I expect we'll finish pretty early, like about midnight or something. Or earlier,' I said, 'if you think we ought. I mean, it's not going to be a rave-up. We'll keep it quite quiet and orderly. I don't expect, probably, there'll even be any dancing or anything.'

'Oh, but there must be dancing! People always have dancing at parties! Don't they? They did when I was your age.'

'Well, yes, but—' If David couldn't dance it didn't seem quite fair; not when the party was being given in his honour.

'You must do just whatever you would normally do,' said Mrs Geary. 'It won't be any fun, otherwise. Besides, if you don't have any dancing David will guess that it's because of him, and then that will make him feel bad, and I know you don't want that.'

'No.' I shook my head: that was the very last thing we wanted.

'So have your music, and your dancing, and just make it a perfectly ordinary, normal party. David will do what he can do, and if there's anything he can't

—well, that's no reason for the rest of you to stop doing it. When I said don't expect too much of him, I didn't mean physically so much as . . . oh! mentally. He can cope with the physical thing; walking and all the rest. That's no problem. But the other—' She stopped. 'It's been terribly difficult for him to come to terms with it, Robyn. If he doesn't seem quite the same David as he used to—well, I'd like to feel that you understand.'

I nodded, vigorously, eager to reassure her. Quoting Mumps, I said, 'You can't expect someone to go through an experience like that and emerge unscathed.' And then, remembering what Pop had told me, 'The drugs can sometimes make people pretty depressed, can't they?'

'Yes. Oh, yes! Indeed they can. They can do more than just make people depressed.'

'I don't like them,' I said.

She looked up, quickly. 'You don't?'

'No. If you ask me—' I was on the point of saying that if you asked me they quite often did more harm than good and that sometimes people were just used as guinea pigs (I'd read that somewhere, in quite a serious sort of book). Just in time I remembered that this was David's mother I was talking to.

'You were saying?' she said.

'Well, it's just that I think, only that's only my opinion, I think they use too many of them. I don't think they ought to be allowed to keep giving them to people the way they do . . . people getting hooked on sleeping tablets and everything. But of course in some cases, I mean where there's no alternative—well, I mean, that's different. Where it's actually going to *achieve* something. I mean it's worth it, then.'

'You're just saying that, aren't you?' said Mrs

137

Geary. 'You're just saying it because I'm David's mother and you feel that you ought.'

'No! It's true! I mean—I've talked about it, I've—'

'Robyn, it's all right.' She laid her hand on mine across the table. 'You don't have to. David isn't going to be having any more chemotherapy.'

'Not—' My mouth dropped open. I felt the bottom of my stomach give a great sick-making lurch. It was ridiculous, when here I'd been, all this time, internally raging at the way the medical profession chucked drugs about right, left and centre, and now when David's mother said he wasn't going to be given any more, when I ought to have been rejoicing I suddenly felt as if the world had come to a stop. 'But what—I mean, how—'

'Robyn! Please!' Her hand tightened over mine. 'Don't get hold of the wrong end of the stick. Just because he isn't having chemotherapy doesn't mean he's not having any treatment at all. He is; but—other kinds of treatment. Different kinds of treatment. We're not giving up—we haven't just abandoned him. Far from it! We'll do everything we possibly can—short of making his life a misery. I won't have that! I've seen too much of it. My own sister—' She stopped. 'Not again! Not ever again! I don't know how much time David has before him, I don't know whether it's a long time or a short time, but whatever it is, I want it to be good: I'm not having him suffer to no purpose.'

'But surely—surely—' I floundered. 'Surely if—'

'If the doctors advise it? Oh, Robyn! Do you think we haven't been into it all most carefully? *Most* carefully! We've read all there is to read, done all the checking up it's possible to do . . . we know what the chances are. And what they're not.'

138

'You mean—' I swallowed. 'You mean they aren't any *better* with drugs?'

'Not really, Robyn. Not in the long run. And there's so much misery to be gone through . . . I couldn't let them do it! Not to my David!'

It shook me, hearing her say that: my David . . . David was *our* David—mine and Abbey's and Zoot's! More Abbey's than ours, perhaps; but ours as well. For the first time I realized, not just as a fact, but as an *emotion*, that David belonged to other people besides us. He had parents, a brother and sister—he was theirs, before he was ours. But we had claims on him too!

Mrs Geary put up a handkerchief and blotched at the corners of her eyes with it.

'Now I've gone and made you cry.' (She had, but she was crying just as much.) 'I'm sorry! I shouldn't have done that—I didn't mean to. I was trying to be positive. That's the word, isn't it? What Abbey said you'd all decided to be? Well, that's what I was being. I see it as a very *positive* thing, the quality of life. Far more positive than survival at no matter what the cost. The cost in some cases is just too high. That's not being positive! That's—'

'It wasn't because of me,' I said, 'was it?'

'Because of you?' She broke off, in surprise. 'My poor Robyn! Why should it be because of you?'

'Because of—of me upsetting him.'

Gently, she said, 'How did you do that?'

'When I'—I took a breath—'smuggled Max in.'

'Oh! Yes.' A smile flitted briefly across her face. 'That!'

'Abbey said that he'd—he'd said he didn't want any more treatment. He just wanted to come home.'

'Yes; he was very disturbed at that period. Not just

139

because of you bringing Max in. Everything. It was a bad time altogether.'

'So it wasn't—I mean, it wasn't—'

'It wasn't *your fault*, if that's what you're thinking. It wasn't anybody's fault—it isn't a fault! It's a decision we came to together; David and his father and I. We talked it out at great length. I do promise you, Robyn, it's not something we decided on lightly . . . I told your father that. He was very good about it. I was grateful to him. Not all doctors would have been.'

'Doctors!' I said. 'What do they know?'

She sighed.

'They do their best, Robyn. They can't work miracles. So long as they're sympathetic . . . sometimes that's the most that one can ask of them.'

As I was wheeling my bike back across the yard, I suddenly thought of something: 'Does Abbey know?'

David's mother nodded.

'Yes,' she said. 'Abbey knows.'

Slowly and soberly, I cycled back home. For my part I was glad David wasn't going to be given any more of their horrid drugs, I'd always hated the thought of it; but Abbey—Abbey had been pinning such faith on them! Only the other day, talking about something quite different—we'd been talking about computers and Little Jane had been complaining about how they were taking over—Abbey had flared up and said she didn't have patience with people who refused to move with the times: we were living in an age of technology, we might just as well accept it and make the most of it. I had a feeling, even then, that she'd been thinking about those wretched drugs.

When I got in, Pop was in the bath.

'Can I come and talk?' I said.

He obviously guessed it was important, because he

didn't groan and say 'If you must' which is what he usually says. (He likes to take a week's supply of newspapers in with him and wallow.)

'You didn't tell me,' I said, 'that David wasn't going to be having treatment any more.'

He lowered his paper and peered at me over the top of it. He looks absurd, lying in the bath with his glasses perched on his nose and *The Times* spread over him. I bet some of his patients wouldn't think him so god-like if they could see him like that.

'Who said David wasn't having treatment any more?'

'His mother! I've just—'

'What did she say, exactly?'

'She said he wasn't having any more chemotherapy. She—'

'Not having any more chemotherapy is not the same as not having treatment any more. God help the unfortunate soul,' said Pop, 'who ever has to rely on *you* to give evidence in court!' He ruffled the sodden pages of his newspaper. 'You really must learn to be more precise.'

He was purposely steering me away from the point.

'You might have told me,' I said. I was aware, even as I said it, that I was sounding like Sophie. I knew how she felt.

'Robyn,' said Pop, 'you have been my daughter for nigh on seventeen years. For every single one of those years I have been a practising GP. If you have not learnt by now—'

'Yes, I know!' I said. 'I know you can't discuss patients, but this is different! I'm not asking you to discuss anything *personal*.'

'If treatment isn't personal, I'd like to know what is!'

'They told Abbey,' I said.

141

'So now they've told you! So what's your grouse?'

'If you'd told me earlier I could have talked about it with her.' I had suddenly realized the significance of that new philosophy of hers: I'm just going to live from day to day . . . 'She was really relying on those drugs. She'd really got it into her head that they were a sort of magic whatdyoumacall it.'

Pop looked at me. I thought he was going to go on again about my lack of precision, but all he said was: 'There is no magic, Robyn, in medicine.'

'Well, *I* know that! I was thinking of Abbey. She really believed in those damned horrible drugs.'

'I would have you know,' said Pop, beginning to bristle, 'that there are people walking round today who owe their lives to those *damned horrible drugs* as you call them.'

'So how do you feel about David not having them?'

Almost imperceptibly, he hunched a shoulder.

'How I feel is immaterial. Once I've made my views known . . . one can only respect the patient's freedom of choice.'

'Yes, but do you *agree* with it? I want to know! I want to know what you think!'

Carefully, he said, 'A doctor naturally likes to use every means at his disposal for the treatment of a patient.'

'So you *don't* agree!'

'I didn't say that.'

'So you *do* agree?'

He hedged. 'It's not that easy. In specific cases—'

'Suppose it were me?' I said. 'What would you say then?'

Pop shook his head.

'Don't ask me, Robyn. I honestly don't know.'

The day of the party arrived. David had come home the previous evening and although Abbey hadn't been out to the farm to see him they'd spoken on the telephone (as they'd spoken nearly every night since he'd been away. Goodness only knows what the telephone bills must have been like: nobody seemed to care). Abbey said that he sounded in good spirits and that he was looking forward to the party.

I was glad about that because we'd worked very hard to ensure its success. Abbey had baked a cake, a huge, rich, fruity one, and Zoot and I had helped her ice it. We hadn't been able to think of a suitable joke, but what we'd done, we'd made this little picture, in different-coloured icing sugars, of a man on a horse with a dog running by his side. None of us was much use at art, so the figures were a bit what you might call primitive—the matchstick school, Zoot said—but we'd taken great care with the colours. We'd done the horse in chocolate, to look like Sable, and the dog in white and tan (it took us ages to get the tan: we had to mix orange and cochineal with just a dash of lemon) and we'd given him a good long nose and sticking-up tail so that David would know it was meant to be Max, and altogether we felt pretty pleased with ourselves. I had also managed to prevail upon Zoot not to invite the *whole* of the cricket team: he'd compromised with half a dozen.

I tried to coax Abbey into discussing what she was going to wear. She seemed to have lost all interest in clothes just lately. It had been understandable while David was in hospital, but as I said, now that he was back he would want to see her looking presentable. (Not that she ever looked anything else, Abbey has a knack that way, but I had to say *some*thing: lack of interest is not positive.)

143

'For goodness' sake!' Abbey turned on me, quite crossly. 'You sound like my mother . . . don't wear trousers, men don't like women in trousers . . . do something with your hair, men like to see nice hair . . . sexist claptrap! You don't imagine David's going to spend hours looking through his wardrobe to find something that turns *me* on, do you?'

As a matter of fact, I thought he very well might.

'I don't see why he shouldn't,' I said.

'Because he doesn't need to! It doesn't matter to me what he looks like. Looks are only superficial. Of course it's different for you, going into a profession where looks are everything.'

'Not *every*thing,' I said. Hadn't she ever heard of talent?

She had; but dismissed it.

'The acting profession,' she said, 'is just so *facile*.'

That smacked to me of Willie.

'It may be facile,' I said, 'but at least people take a pride in how they look. There's nothing to be gained from going round like some old boot.'

I think my words must have sunk in, because when Abbey arrived on Saturday (she came early, with Zoot, on Zoot's cousin's motorbike, to help me prepare) she was wearing this really fabulous get-up that I'd never seen before: a long, swirly skirt of Indian cotton, a top of the same material (with a nice expanse of flesh in between) and silver thonged sandals. She was also wearing The Ring—the one that Zoot had won at Sophie's hoopla and had given to David. I didn't comment on the Indian cotton (not wishing to be thought to crow) but I did on the ring.

'You're wearing Zoot's bauble!' I said.

'Yes. Well—' She gave a little laugh; obviously embarrassed. 'It goes with things.'

It did, I had to admit it—the Indian cotton was a deep, dark blue, and so was the stone in Zoot's ring. But somehow I didn't feel that that was the reason she was wearing it.

'That bauble,' said Zoot, 'was given to your beloved.'

'Her beloved,' I said, 'obviously gave it to her.'

'But I gave it to him as an *engagement* bauble.'

'So maybe he gave it to her as an eng—'

'Look, why don't you two shut up,' said Abbey, 'and start doing something useful?'

The party well repaid our efforts. As I'd told Mrs Geary, it wasn't a rave-up—but it *was* a success. David came with Ned, in the car. (We invited Ned to stay, but he said, 'Best not; he'll only think I'm spying on him. Besides, I wouldn't want to cramp your style . . . all you young things!' Anyone would have thought Ned was ancient: he was only twenty-*four*.)

David was looking gorgeous. He'd obviously spent the whole of the last fortnight out of doors, because he had this terrific suntan. I was even more glad than before that I'd nagged at Abbey to dress up. Even I had dressed up a little—I'd bought myself some baggy pants, red silk, and a purple blouse to go with them —and *I* didn't have anyone special to dress up for.

Zoot was in sweat shirt and jeans as usual. (I have *never* seen Zoot in formal attire. I believe he may once have possessed a school tie, but if so that is about all.) The Janes were there, Big Jane looking like a butter mountain in yellow, Little Jane like a strawberry in pink. Andy came, and was also in pink. Pink suited Andy; it made him look almost fanciable. He danced quite a lot with Little Jane. I danced quite a lot with Pilch. Pilch was wearing his tight trousers—Pilch always wears tight trousers—and a shirt that was

145

open all the way down to the navel. Very sexy. (Very butch.) In the old days Zoot and David would have taken the piss, but we'd all grown out of that by now.

I also danced a bit with Zoot, though Zoot isn't the most enthusiastic of dancers. Abbey didn't dance with anyone at all until just right at the end when Con Masters, who was in the cricket team, persuaded her. Con was really nice, but so were some of the others and none of them had been able to talk her round. I think she only did it because of Con being the sole black student in the whole of our year (you don't get many black people in Clearhaven—you don't get many of anything save porky pink English) and Abbey, who is sensitive to people's feelings, not wanting him to feel slighted. Silly, really, because I'm pretty sure he only asked her for the same reason, not liking to see her left out. She'd spent all evening sitting with David. She told me later—weeks later—that she'd asked him whether he felt like dancing, and he'd said no, but not to let that stop her; but being Abbey, of course, it *had* stopped her—until Con came along. And that introduced the one sour note of the evening. Not because of what Abbey did, but because of what David did.

We had in our year at Clareville a girl called Stephanie Barber. Steph was one of those who just can't help giving what Pop, in his quaint old-fashioned way, likes to call 'the glad eye'. She doesn't have to do anything: it's just this image that she projects. I mean, she just is naturally a very sexy sort of person. Zoot and David, chauvinist pigs that they were, used to refer to her as 'The Bicycle', and quite a few of the girls didn't like her, saying that she was nympho, which actually was a gross libel: Steph was nothing if not selective.

146

Abbey and I had always got on pretty well with her (hence the invitation to the party) though maybe that was only because she'd never done any poaching on our particular property. Well, I'd never really had any property to be poached on, Zoot and I being strictly mates; and nobody, but *nobody*, would have tried it on with David. Not until that evening at the party. Because while Abbey was dancing with Con, Steph Barber actually went up to David, hauled him to his feet, and dragged him with her into the middle of the room. It was practically rape. The only thing that stopped it being so was that after the first few seconds of looking awkward David began to let go and quite obviously to enjoy himself. It wouldn't have been so bad except that Steph's idea of dancing (by the time it gets to midnight) is to loop herself round her partner's neck and blood-suck like a leech. I was torn between being glad to see David dancing at all and furious to see him doing it with anyone other than Abbey. I thought that was really mean of him.

It was next morning, when we were talking things over at the breakfast table, that Mumps came up with something which made sense. She was asking me about the party, how it had gone and whether David had enjoyed himself. I said I thought he had, on the whole.

'Only on the whole?' said Mumps.

I explained that he'd seemed a bit subdued, not quite as outgoing as usual—there hadn't been any daftness, or fooling around with Zoot—but we agreed that that was hardly to be wondered at. But then I told her about the dancing: how poor old Abbey had sat there at his side all night only to have that rat Stephanie come up and snitch him at the last moment.

'I do think that was rotten of him,' I said, 'don't you?'

Mumps thought about it, then said: 'I take it this Stephanie is a bit of a hustler?'

I said that she could say *that* again.

'Well, but sometimes,' said Mumps, 'even hustlers have their uses. You have to remember that David was probably feeling very self-conscious—he needed someone to come along and bully him. It's a hard lesson, but one that I'm afraid Abbey is going to have to learn . . . there is such a thing as being *too* considerate.'

I thought upon reflection that she was very likely right.

9

David was back at school for the last few weeks of term. Everybody said how terribly well he was doing, meaning how well he was coping, not being depressed or self-pitying, just getting on with things, and I suppose it was true; I suppose he was. I didn't see as much of him as I would normally have done on account of rehearsals taking up almost every spare minute of my time. When I did see him, however, he seemed almost his old self. I even noticed him in the nets on one occasion, letting Zoot bowl at him.

His relationship with the Windbag was interesting, because if anyone was *not* his old self it was the Great Rhetorical. When David first came back he treated him with what I can only describe as exaggerated caution: none of the usual scintillating sarcasm or flow of wit. I remember there was a short period, just for a day or two, when David had to use crutches (I can't now recall why: some temporary problem which cleared up) and the Great Rhetorical, not realizing, asked him to come out front and chair this debate. I remember David playing it for all it was worth—'Aargh, Jim lad! Now for me famous Long John Silver impersonation!' —and everybody laughing (because if David laughed, then how could you not?) except for the Great Rhetorical. The Great Rhetorical was really thrown: it was the first time I'd ever seen him at a loss. But then, after a week or two, even he had recovered and was back to being his normal rebarbative self, which I think was the way David probably preferred it.

At weekends Abbey went out to the farm and I

suppose either Ned or Mr Geary gave her a lift back at night, or maybe she actually slept there. I was so bound up with *Much Ado* that I didn't really take a lot of notice of what was happening in the outside world. I do remember that at that time Zoot was going through a motorbike phase, because once or twice when we wanted him for Sunday rehearsals he grumbled mightily at being asked to give up his precious weekend to mouthing Shakespeare when he could have been out biking.

Not until the actual performances—we did three: one on the Friday, two on the Saturday—had come and gone did I really swim back to the surface and take note of what was going on around me. What was going on was not as satisfactory as I had lulled myself into believing. Everyone, and that included Mumps, was still commenting on the fact that David was doing 'so marvellously well'. Mumps met him at the Saturday evening performance. She said to me the next day that she could hardly believe it.

'It's quite remarkable, the way he's adjusted.'

I thought she meant physically, so I said, 'Yes, I know,' because I agreed with her, I thought it was absolutely incredible, the fact that he could come back to school and that even now a whole lot of the kids, the ones that weren't in our year and didn't really have that much to do with us, didn't actually *know*; because apart from slopes and stairs, which he couldn't manage too well, you'd just have thought he had a bit of a stiff leg, like when Big Jane had had water on the knee and had been done up in a crêpe bandage for weeks. But then Mumps said she hadn't just meant physically, but emotionally, and I didn't say anything to that. Mumps hadn't seen him afterwards, after the performances, at the party that we held on stage. He had been so unkind to Abbey, and not just once, either.

First was when he was congratulating me on my performance as Beatrice. After he'd told me how good I was (and I'd tried my best to play modest and hadn't succeeded, because I *do* like praise when I know it's deserved) Abbey added her bit. She said, 'Honestly, Robyn, it was great! I take it all back, what I said the other day . . . I couldn't get up there and do what you did. Not in a million years!'

'Well, of course you couldn't,' said David. 'You have to be outgoing, you have to be prepared to take risks. Nobody who pussyfoots through life could ever hope to be an actress.'

Poor Abbey! She went bright red—I felt so sorry for her. It was such a mean thing to say. It was unfair, too: Abbey doesn't pussyfoot. It's true she tends to be cautious—no one would call her impulsive, which is what I'm always accused of being—but it's certainly not true that she isn't prepared to take risks. Heavens! Every time you go on a demo you're putting yourself in the firing line, and Abbey has never flinched from *that*.

I remember I did my best to gloss over the situation, trying to cover up David's beastliness (it was so un*like* him) by hauling in Zoot as a sort of rescue mission, but I could see that Abbey had been hurt. At the same time she didn't seem awfully surprised, so that I couldn't help wondering whether this sort of thing had occurred before.

It was while Zoot was dutifully, at my insistence, regaling them with a funny story about something that had happened in the boys' dressing room before the performance, that David perpetrated his second act of beastliness. Quite suddenly, in the middle of the story, which actually *was* quite amusing, he called out,

'Hey! There's my favourite serving wench!' and without the least word of apology detached himself from us and peeled off across stage to talk to Steph Barber, who was still wearing her make-up and therefore looking rather more glamorous than the rest of us, who had scrubbed ourselves clean with Crowe's Cremine. (All she'd been playing was one of Hero's henchwomen. Nothing whatsoever to write home about.) She and David spent the next ten minutes openly flirting. Openly making *eyes* at each other. I did my best to ignore it, on the grounds that if you pretend something isn't happening then maybe nobody else will notice, but it was quite obvious that Abbey had. Well, she couldn't really have missed it; not the way they were carrying on. I felt absolutely furious with David.

Over the next few days I began to notice more and more that his behaviour towards Abbey left a lot, as Willie once remarked on my behaviour in her physics classes, to be desired. He seemed intent on putting her down all the time. Whatever she suggested, he would sneer at: whatever she said, he would mock. Looking back, I realized that he had always had a slight tendency towards the cavalier in his treatment of her. I remember thinking once or twice in the past that Abbey put up with more than she ought. But he'd never been unkind to her, which was what he was being now.

We arranged (it being summer holidays) to go one evening to Brighton together, just the four of us. We didn't want Pilch and Andy, or the Janes; we didn't want a group thing. We wanted it to be just us, DavidnAbbey, me and Zoot, as it had in the past.

Of course, you never *can* re-create things that have gone; I know that now. I didn't realize it then. We tried very hard—it almost worked. We strolled along the sea front eating candy floss and wearing funny hats: we went on the pier and played the slot machines: we did a round of clock golf on the green. We didn't go on the Dodgems, as once we would have done, and we didn't get our fortunes told, but they weren't the things that ruined it. What ruined it was Abbey and me catching sight of a cinema showing this all-Walt Disney programme for the kids.

'Cor, look!' I said. '*Pinocchio!*'

'And *Snow White!*' Abbey was ecstatic. 'I loved *Snow White!*'

We looked at each other, eagerly.

'Shall we go?'

Abbey and I wanted to: Zoot and David didn't. They started coming on all heavy and he-man—'*Pinocchio*? Snow *White*? Leave it out!' They were really quite objectionable. In the end, Abbey said, 'Well, we're going to go! You two can do what you like.'

'The best idea you've had all day,' said David. 'We'll do our thing: you do yours.'

There had once been a time when it would never have occurred to David to go off and do his own thing without Abbey. We would all have gone to the cinema, and David and Abbey would have sat and held hands and indulged in kissing sessions, while Zoot and I would have touched shoulders, and just occasionally knees, which would have given us both a bit of a buzz without actually rousing us to any deeper depths of passion. But it would have been fun. Now Abbey and I sat there, while Zoot and David went rollicking off round Brighton on their own.

'What'll you do?' I asked them; but in lordly fashion they told me not to worry: they would find 'something'.

I was the one who hesitated at letting them go off. It was Abbey who seemed suddenly determined to do *her* own thing, whether with David or without him. I thought probably she had had just about as much as she could take, and I couldn't really say that I blamed her. David *could* be pig-like when he wanted. We arranged to meet them at ten o'clock, when the programme finished.

'And don't be late,' I said.

David jerked his thumb.

'Who does she think she is? Issuing her orders . . . Lady Nevershit?'

'Do you mind?' Abbey glared at him. There were kids going in, accompanied by their parents. Some of them were starting to look at us rather curiously. Abbey seized me by the arm. 'Let's go!'

As we walked through the doors we were treated to the full blast of Zoot's tuneless baritone, foghorning after us: 'Ladies Johnson and Mather, Get all in a lather, When someone says sh—' Fortunately, at that point, the doors closed and we heard no more. There were times when Zoot and David could really be an embarrassment.

Abbey and I didn't say much while we were in the cinema. What little was said, was said by me, and was mostly on the lines of 'I wonder what they're up to?' 'I wonder what they're doing?' 'I just hope they're *there.*'

They were there—waiting for us on the beach, at the spot we had designated. The only trouble was, they were drunk: drunk and wet. They had been, Zoot explained, for a paddle.

'Paddle inna sea.'

To which David charmingly added the information that they had had a piddle as well as a paddle—'piddle *an*na paddle'—to which Zoot said, 'Ooh, lovely!' at which they collapsed against each other in foolish giggles (being sprawled out at our feet on the stones). Abbey and I stood, looking down at them.

'You've been drinking!' I said.

I'd never seen Zoot and David drunk before—come to that, I don't believe they'd ever *been* drunk before. It really made them quite stupid. They rolled about giggling, soaking wet and totally irresponsible. They kept making these asinine remarks, which I suppose they thought were amusing, and bawling 'the Ladies Johnson and Mather' at the tops of their voices.

'Just listen to them,' I said to Abbey. 'The very acme of wit.'

This, of course, only creased them still further.

'Just listen to them,' piped David, 'the very acne of wit!'

Zoot put his nose in the air and started sniffing.

'Did someone say shit?'

They liked that. It kept them happy for several minutes, just saying the word and making obscene suggestions.

'You know your trouble?' I said. 'You're drunk!'

Howls, hoots, and raucous raspberries.

'You're drunk! You're drunk!'

'I knew we shouldn't have let them go off.'

'I knew we shouldn't have let them g—'

'Oh, shut up!' I said. 'You're foul!'

How cross we were with them! All tight-lipped and prudish, me as well as Abbey. In fact, of the two, I think I was the more tight-lipped. Abbey actually took it quite well. She was quite tolerant. I was the one, kneeling stiff-backed and outraged on a patch of sand, who railed at them—yet it was poor old Abbey who came in for most of the stick. All she said, crouched at

155

David's side, was, 'Look, just try and pull yourselves together, will you, and sober up? It's time we were catching our train.'

They parodied her, instantly.

'Tame we was ketchin our trane—'

'Well, it is,' said Abbey.

'It is!'

'It is!'

'And stop repeating everything! You're like a couple of children.'

That really got them.

'Ooh, naughty!'

'Naughty boys!'

'Pore ole Abbey! Gotta knockers inna—'

'*Knickers* inna—'

'Knockers inna—'

Abbey looked at me and pulled an exasperated face; and at that moment David, owlish, said: 'Can't be! Hasn't got 'ny.'

'Got 'ny wot?' said Zoot.

'Knockers.'

Zoot frowned.

'Abbey's got knockers! Got nice li'l knockers . . . go 'n a champagne glass, Abbey's knockers.'

'Don' like knockers that'd go 'n a champagne glass. I like *big* knockers. Knockers like Robyn's.'

'Robyn's is like puddin' basins . . . puddin' basin knockers.'

I drew the line at that; I really did. It was one thing being drunk, quite another having them refer to a part of my anatomy as pudding basins. I didn't see why I should sit there and be abused, and I didn't see why Abbey should, either. I just couldn't understand why David had taken to being so hateful to her. Abbey of all people didn't deserve such treatment.

'She's such a good girl. She's been so brave, so . . . mature.'

It was his own mother who had said it. She ought to know.

But I remembered, also, what Mumps had said: 'There is such a thing as being *too* considerate.' I wondered, that night on the beach, whether that was what Abbey was being. The beach at Brighton is all pebbles; it would almost certainly have given David problems even if he hadn't been drunk. Being drunk, he found it impossible. Had *I* been Abbey I would have left him to get on with it: Abbey being Abbey has to try and help. And of course she can't, can she? She's not strong enough. If anything, she just makes matters worse. So there we are, stuck on Brighton beach at 10.30 at night, me furious, Abbey ineffectual, Zoot and David high as kites and David incapable of taking more than one step in any direction without falling over and being unable to get up again.

Looking back on it now, I am full of understanding and compassion. It makes me feel dreadful. At the time I could express nothing but rage.

'Look, if he got *down* here—'

'Oh, Robyn, don't!' begged Abbey.

'Well, but I'm just saying . . . if he got *down*, for goodness' sake, he ought to be able to get *up*. Coming down's harder than going up. How did he *get* down?'

'I don't know! They probably weren't so drunk then, or Zoot helped him, or—'

'Zoot!' I marched up to Zoot and grabbed him by the hair, yanking his face towards me.

'Wot?' said Zoot.

'Stop behaving like a drunken hyena and help David get back up that beach!'

Zoot blinked.

'Yes, ma'am!'

It was the only way to do it: you *had* to bully them. It was the only thing they would respond to.

We were oddly quiet on the journey home. Zoot and David sat together, lolling against each other, Abbey and I sat opposite, prim and purse-lipped. Normally, at the other end, David and I would have caught a bus: that night we got a cab. We left Abbey, rather sadly, going off in one direction, Zoot reeling away in the other. In the cab, David tried it on a bit with me. I thought of all those times when I'd wondered how it would be to be kissed by him. Now, when I could have found out, I had to stop it happening. It would have been a betrayal of Abbey; and anyway, I knew he was only doing it because of being drunk.

When I complained to Mumps, which I did as soon as I got in, about disgusting ug-like behaviour on the part of piss-sodden males (I didn't say anything about David trying it on in the cab) she just laughed and said, 'Oh, Robyn! Don't be so prissy. They've got to be allowed their bit of fun once in a while.' I didn't mind them having fun, but I did object to them ruining our evening. And I *did* object to David being beastly to Abbey.

A few days later, Abbey went off on holiday with her parents. They went every year, and every year to the same place: up to Cumbria, to stay with relations. Last year, David had gone with them. This year, I suppose because he wasn't really up to rock-climbing and hill work, Abbey went by herself. I suppose that was the reason. Abbey didn't mention it, and I didn't ask. I sensed that she wasn't terribly looking forward to going. We sat and discussed it over a pizza in Larry's the day before she left. She said she'd really be glad to get back and to get started on a new term. I knew what she meant: I think we both wanted the happenings of the last few months to be well and truly behind us.

'And Christmas is always my favourite.'

'Mine, too,' I said. The Christmas term really was the best one of all. It started with a bang, with the sixth form social, held on the first Saturday of term (strictly for sixth years: none of your fifth form rubbish). This year it was to be a Viennese evening, with the school orchestra providing the music. Then, in October, there was Hallowe'en, which we traditionally made a big thing of, followed by fireworks night, and carol singing, and the pantomime—

'Hey!' I said, suddenly excited. 'I wonder if we really *could* do *Treasure Island*? The kids would love it—all that blood and guts! On the other hand'—I thought about it a bit more—'it's horribly sexist. There isn't one decent woman's part in the whole thing. Maybe we could do *Peter Pan*? Then I could be Peter!'

Abbey looked at me.

'Well, I mean I could if I was offered it,' I said. 'Naturally there'd have to be auditions. But David would make a smashing Captain Hook, and Zoot and Pilch could be Pirates, and Little Jane could be Wendy, and—'

'Are you going to the social with Pilch?' said Abbey.

'What?' The question threw me. Why should Abbey think I was going with Pilch? She didn't bother waiting for my reply.

'I don't think I'll be going,' she said. 'David doesn't want to.'

'Why's that?'

'Oh, Robyn!' Her tone was reproachful. It said, quite plainly, do I have to spell it out for you? 'What fun would it be for him, if he can't join in?'

It maybe wouldn't be fun for David, but it could still be fun for Abbey. And as David's mother had said, David will do what he can do, and if there's anything he can't—well, that was no reason for the rest of us to stop doing it.

'Just because he doesn't want to go,' I said, 'doesn't mean you can't.'

I had uttered treason: if David didn't want to go, then Abbey wouldn't dream of doing so. Not even though it was she, originally, who'd put forward the idea of a Viennese evening, she who'd helped organize it, helped choose the music, discussed with me (way back in the spring) what we should both wear. She'd even gone out, I remember, and bought some lengths of material for a dress she was planning to make. I wondered if she had actually made it, and if so, when she would ever get around to wearing it.

Again, I thought: there is such a thing as being *too* considerate. But I didn't say so. I knew Abbey too well.

10

The same weekend that Abbey went away, there was a party. It was given by a friend of a friend of somebody, and I went there with Pilch, who rang me at the last moment to say that he'd just heard about it and did I feel like going? Since I didn't have anything else to do, I thought I might as well. There was Abbey up in Cumbria, Zoot off on some bike rally, David—David presumably doing his own thing, whatever that was. He and I never went out together when Abbey was away. He'd quite often do things with Zoot, but biking didn't interest him. I guessed he'd be out at the farm communing with Sable, playing with Max: just happy to be back with his beloved animals. I arranged with Pilch that he would pick me up at eight o'clock in his mother's car.

The party (it was held in a squat in a semi-derelict house down by the docks, near to where Zoot lived) really wasn't terribly good. It was gatecrashed quite early on by a load of zombies who took up residence in the middle of the floor and just sat there, smoking pot, so at eleven o'clock, when nothing much seemed to be happening, or likely to happen, Pilch and I lit out. We went to Larry's first, for a couple of pizzas, which Pilch insisted on paying for—I did offer to go halves, but Pilch said he was flush at the moment on account of his holiday job, life-saving at the local baths—and then he asked me if I'd care for a walk along the beach. I said yes, all right; why not?

I reflected, as we wandered by the water's edge, on the ironies of life. A year ago, I had been sprawled on that same stretch of beach with Abbey and the others, happily making mock (not that Abbey ever did) as Pilch and Andy went past. I could still remember catcalling, and David and Zoot singing their Andy Pandy song. Now here I was hand in hand with Pilch beneath the moonlight, feeling almost romantic. So many things had changed from a year ago. Some for better; some—some I didn't want to think about. Not tonight.

We had just reached the pier—a piddling affair, not at all like the one at Brighton—and I was debating with myself whether or not to walk under it, because walking under Clearhaven pier with a boy is very nearly the same as offering yourself to him, I mean unless you're totally naïve it's accepted as one of the signals, when we saw that a couple were already there. They were lying on the ground, half hidden by one of the wooden support pillars: they were Steph Barber and David.

I couldn't help seeing. I wished that I hadn't, but the moon was full on them. They saw us, as well. We had gone too far for anyone to pretend. Pilch, doing his hearty bit, said, 'And a walloping good time was had by all!' Steph just smiled sweetly and said nothing. David, obviously abashed, struggled to sit up. (He had to struggle, on account of having arms and legs all wrapped around him.)

'We've just been for a swim,' he said.

I, like Steph, didn't say anything. I might as well admit it, I was embarrassed. Embarrassed at seeing David like that, embarrassed at seeing him with Steph, embarrassed just at *seeing* him. David, who once had been my hero, whom once I had dreamed about . . . David on the beach with Stephanie Barber . . .

Pilch and I walked on, skirting the edge of the pier,

up the steps, along the prom, back to where he had parked his mother's car.

'Sorry about that,' said Pilch.

Why should Pilch be sorry? What did he have to apologize for? He wasn't the one who had been caught beneath the pier, rolling about half naked.

'It's just one of those things,' he said. He squeezed my hand. 'It happens.'

I was only thankful that I didn't have to face Abbey.

I wouldn't have been surprised to have had a telephone call from David the next day (guilty conscience and all that) but in fact it was over a week later when he got in touch. One thing I had been determined not to do and that was to get in touch with *him*. When he did finally call I was irritated to note that he didn't sound in the least bit ashamed, or conscious of having done anything wrong. On the contrary, he sounded positively *jaunty*.

'What are you up to?' he said.

I felt a strong temptation to tell him that whatever I was up to, it wasn't any business of his. Instead (because when all was said and done, David was still David) I said, 'Nothing very much. How about you?' I nearly added, 'Crawled out from under the pier at last?' The only reason I didn't is because mostly one doesn't: one can never quite bring oneself. But I had to say *some*thing. So what I said was, 'Heard from Abbey?'

'Of course!'

What did he mean, *of course*? He had a nerve, taking things for granted!

'I'm so glad,' I said. Glacial; positively glacial. What Zoot would have called my brass-monkey voice. (What I call my Lady Bracknell voice.) I might just as well not have bothered: it went right over his head. All he said was, 'Heard from her yesterday. Want to come for a walk?'

I was still such an idiot where David was concerned. I should have asked him where Stephanie was, or told him that I was otherwise engaged. The most I managed was a grudging, 'Where?'

'Down the beach.'

I thought about it. (Of course I had every intention of going.)

'I suppose I *could*.'

I said it as ungraciously as possible, just to remind him that I was far from happy with him, but once again it sailed right over.

'Do you good,' he said.

'I don't need doing good!'

'Yes, you do. Can't stuff indoors on a day like this. I'll meet you down Bingham's in one hour.'

I said, '*Bing*ham's?' We hadn't been to Bingham's in ages. It was a rather seedy sea-front café at the foot of Bingham's Wharf, where once we had been in the habit of congregating. We'd given it up principally because of David: it's approached by a steep slope, which is often quite slippy. We'd known, after his operation, that he wouldn't be able to manage it, so we'd simply stopped going.

'One hour,' said David. 'OK?'

I shrugged. If he wanted to fall over and break his neck . . . I was still extremely angry with him. I'd had a card from Abbey only that morning, all innocent and happy, saying how much she was looking forward to getting back—and *what did she have to get back to*? A boyfriend who rolled about under the pier with other women. I made up my mind, as I went in on the bus, that I would let my displeasure be felt. I would be very

164

cold and cutting, and (when I could think of any) would make Cryptic Comments such as would leave him in no doubt that I knew perfectly well what he had been up to.

The first cryptic comment I thought I would make was, 'Been for any good swims recently?' I sat on the bus rehearsing it in varying shades of meaning. I planned to greet him with it, but as is the way with even the best-laid plans it all went for naught because the sight that met my eyes quite killed any immediate desire for recrimination: David was down on the beach with Max, throwing pebbles. He had not only safely negotiated the slope, but was actually galloping about.

'Hey!' I yelled. 'That's great!'

I catapulted down the slope towards him. David turned, and grinned, and took a mock bow.

'I thank you! Not quite as good as Mark I, perhaps, but a decided improvement on Mark II . . . '

'When did they fit it?'

'Monday.'

'That's fantastic! Does Zoot know?'

'Not yet. You're the first to be honoured.'

'What about Abbey?'

'Oh, well, yes,' he said. 'Abbey.'

That at least was something. I wondered why she hadn't mentioned it to me, because presumably she must have known before she went away, but I thought most likely she'd been too bound up with other matters. And that reminded me: I was supposed to be showing my displeasure.

It's not so easy, showing displeasure to someone who's just been given a new leg, Mark III, and is obviously pretty chuffed about it. You have to be a bit of a louse. There was only one way to do it, and that was by thinking very hard of Abbey.

'So,' I said, 'what shall we do?' (Even then I felt rotten; but he *had* treated her badly.) 'Go for a swim?'

'Can't; haven't got any trunks with me. Let's have an ice-cream. Fancy an ice-cream?'

'Yes, please,' I said. 'Strawberry. I'm surprised you didn't bring them, now that you can swim again.'

He didn't say anything to that; just concentrated on buying three strawberry ice-creams (one for me, one for himself, one for Max).

'I've got mine,' I said.

'Your what?'

'Bikini. Under my shorts.'

'So you go for a swim! I'll sit and watch.'

'But it's more fun when you both do it.' I licked, lecherously, at my ice-cream. 'You did it with Steph,' I said.

I had the satisfaction (if that was what it was) of seeing him grow slightly red.

'It was dark then.'

'Would you do it with me if it were dark?'

He looked at me, uncertainly.

'Go swimming with you?'

What did he think?

'Like you did with Steph.'

'Yes,' he said. 'Of course.'

'But only if it were dark.'

He frowned.

'Not in daylight? Not when—'

'Oh, pack it in, Robyn!' He tossed the end of his ice-cream cone for Max. 'Don't push me, I can't cope with everything all at once.'

'Well, but if you didn't mind with *Steph*anie,' I said.

'I don't mind with you. It's other people.'

166

I shrugged.

'So what can they do? Only stare.'

'So maybe I don't want to be stared at! Stop nagging.'

Abbey would throttle me, I thought, if she were here. Well, but she wasn't here! I, too, tossed the end of my ice-cream cone for Max. Abbey wasn't here and *some*one had to speak for her.

'At least now,' I said, 'you'll be able to go to the social.'

'A *Viennese* evening?'

'Why not?'

'Because the big bull dyke in Physio doesn't happen to include ballroom dancing on the agenda! She's taught me how to get on buses, she's taught me how to go upstairs, she's even taught me how to get in the poxy *bath*. But one thing she hasn't taught me, and that's how to do the sodding foxtrot. So I don't really see,' said David, heavily sarcastic, 'what the point of it would be.'

I could tell that I was getting up his nose, but I didn't care. I was thinking of Abbey. She had rights, too.

'The point,' I said, 'is that *Abbey* would like to go. And don't try saying that just because you don't want to it doesn't mean that she can't, because you know perfectly well she won't go without you!'

'That's just stupid.'

'It may be stupid, but at least it's loyal! And stop referring to people as dykes.'

'Why?'

'Because it's sexist, that's why.'

'So if I want to be sexist, I shall be!'

'You *are*,' I said.

We walked on, rather huffily, to the breakwater. It

was the same breakwater that we had sat on, Pilch and Andy, the two Janes, Zoot and Abbey and me, dabbling our toes in the water, at the end of Guild Day. Now I sat on it with David, throwing stones at the incoming tide.

'Are you mad at me,' said David, 'for trying it on with you?'

I was surprised, the state he'd been in, that he remembered.

'Saying I'd got big knockers,' I said.

'Oh!' He grinned. He actually had the cheek. 'So it was that that got you!'

'Not just that. Not that in itself. All the other stuff.'

'What other stuff?'

'Everything! The way you're so mean to Abbey all the time.'

That hit home. He said, 'I'm not mean to her all the time!' but it totally lacked conviction.

'You are,' I said. 'You know you are. Always putting her down and sneering at her. As if she's an idiot, as if she hasn't any brain—'

'Abbey's got brain!'

'Well, don't tell *me*. It's you—it's the way you treat her! Deliberately trying to make her feel small.'

'I don't!'

'Yes, you do! You always did, even before you got—'

I stopped. I had been going to say, before you got ill, but thought perhaps that was being a bit too brutal. David stepped in, to finish it for me.

'Before I got cancer?' he said.

I swallowed. Nobody had ever actually said that word before. I wished he hadn't.

'What's the matter?' He looked at me. 'One might as well be honest: that's what I've got.'

168

'What you *had*,' I said.

He hunched a shoulder; as if the point were academic. 'What you're trying to tell me is that I've always been beastly to Abbey and now I'm being even beastlier.'

'I didn't say you'd been beastly' (though I did think he had) 'but going out with *Stephanie!*'

He hurled a stone, rather viciously, for Max.

'I might have known you'd bring that up!'

'Well, it was rotten,' I said. 'It was a lousy, horrible thing to do!'

'What? Just going for a swim?'

I could have hit him; I really could. I could have *bashed* him.

'Nobody goes swimming with a bicycle,' I said.

'Oh! Oh!' He turned, and jeered. 'Now who's being sexist? Now who's got her claws out?'

'Listen, you!' When Zoot behaved like a thug (which Zoot quite frequently did) I just used to fall on him and thump: I'd never quite had the same free and easy relationship with David. I settled, instead, for jabbing him in the chest with my forefinger. '*You* were the one who started calling her that! *You* were the one who said she went like a bunny rabbit! *You* were the one—'

'Yes, all right!' he said. 'All right!'

'You once said that guys only went with Steph Barber for one thing; remember? You said—'

'I know what I said!'

'So you made a mistake? She's not like that? Mummy's little girl?'

He was silent.

'I just don't see why you had to do it!' I said.

Slowly he bent and picked up a stone; weighed it in his hand, turned it over a couple of times.

'I suppose, because'—he flung the stone: Max,

169

joyous, went hurtling in pursuit—'because I wanted to experience it just once before I die.'

For a moment, I was too shocked to speak. When at last I managed to stammer, 'You're not going to die!' Max had already come charging back to deposit the stone at David's feet.

'I expect I shall,' said David. 'People mostly do. And anyway'—he bent, to retrieve the stone—'I was told that I would.'

I stared at him, the blood running chill in my veins.

'Who t-told you that you would?'

'That fortune teller,' said David. 'Don't you remember? That day we went to Brighton.'

'Oh! That!'

Relief flooded over me: so *that* was all he meant. I did remember the fortune teller. I remembered this fat old crone sitting in her beach hut with a (plastic) crystal ball telling me that I would 'ride the big horses' and me taking it to mean bright lights and leading parts in the West End. I remembered that Abbey's had had something to do with rainbows and that Zoot's was 'seek and ye shall find'. I couldn't remember what David's had been. And then I remembered that that was because he hadn't told us.

'What exactly did she say?' I asked him.

'Gather ye rosebuds.'

I wrinkled my brow. 'Just that?'

'Isn't that enough? "Gather ye rosebuds while ye may, Old time is still a-flying: And this same flower that smiles today Tomorrow will be dying".'

David wasn't really what you would call a poetry buff. (Neither am I.) I knew that he must have gone away and scoured the *Oxford Book of English Verse* in order to find where the lines came from. It was exactly what I did, later. I discovered that it was a poem by

170

Thomas Herrick. It was called 'To Virgins, to Make Much of Time' and I bet it wasn't about dying at all, but about sex. I bet what Herrick was really saying to all these virgins was 'How about it?' nudge nudge, wink wink. They were always on about sex, those old boys: Donne, and Wyatt, and the rest. The metaphysicals, Mrs Hall called them. They were all about sex.

Unfortunately, talking to David on the beach, I didn't realize that because I didn't know who had written his particular poem. So all I could think of to say was, 'You can't believe in *fortune* tellers! You might just as well believe in tea leaves or—or astrology!'

'Some people do,' said David.

'Not if they've got any sense,' I said. And then, trying to make light of it: 'It still isn't any excuse for having it off with Steph!'

Again, he fell silent.

'What I don't understand,' I said, 'what I don't understand—if that was what you wanted—I don't understand why you didn't—well! With Abbey.'

Still, David said nothing.

'I mean, you only had to ask her,' I said. 'She'd let you do anything you want.'

'Yes.' He bent his head. 'I know.'

'So why didn't you?' I thought of poor old Abbey, up in Cumbria, counting the very hours until she could come back to him—and all he could think of to do was roll around with a slag like Steph. (I didn't really think she was a slag. It was just that I was so furious on Abbey's behalf.) 'I mean, she loves you!' I said. 'She'd do anything for you. If you knew—if you only *knew*—what she's been through these last weeks!'

'I do know.'

'Then why?' I said. '*Why?*'

171

There was another long silence.

'I mean, goodness, if it's because of—well, because of your leg,' I said, 'then that's just crazy! Abbey wouldn't care two straws. It wouldn't make the slightest bit of difference to *her*.'

'It mightn't to Abbey,' he said.

But it would to him?

'It didn't seem to bother you with Steph,' I said.

'That was different.'

'Yes! Steph doesn't care about you—Abbey does!'

For just a moment I thought he was going to say something; but then, abruptly, he slid down from the breakwater and without a word began to stride off along the beach.

'David?' Hastily, I sprang down after him. 'David!' I called. 'Wait!'

He slowed his pace slightly as I caught up with him.

'I'm sorry!' I said. 'I didn't mean—'

'It's all right.'

'But I didn't mean to upset you! It's just—'

'It's all *right*.'

It was only then that I realized: for the second time I had gone and done it. Oh, Jesus, I thought! If Abbey were here now . . . she would never forgive me. She always did say that I was obtuse: that I pushed people too hard and never knew when to stop.

'David—'

He reached out and took my hand.

'Don't worry about it.'

'But—'

'Robyn!' He shook his head. 'Don't.'

How could I help it? All I ever seemed to do was put my foot in things. Abbey was right: I *was* obtuse. Me, who observed—me, who was going to be an actress. I should have guessed that all his fooling and joking was only a cover-up. I should have seen. He obviously felt far more deeply about what had been done to him than he ever let on. But that didn't excuse *me*.

Quite suddenly, he stopped.

'Look, I will go to the social,' he said. 'I promise I will. But there's j—'

'No!' I said. 'It's all right! You don't have to! Forget I said it! Forget—'

'Robyn—'

'Forget I ever mentioned it! It doesn't matter! It's not—'

'Robyn, you nerd! Will you just *shut up and let me speak*?'

I gulped.

'Y-yes,' I said. 'S-sorry.'

'Thank you! Now, if you'll just *listen*, all I was going to say was that since you were the one that pushed me into it you can jolly well be the one who teaches me how to dance! There's not much point in going if I can't do anything, is there?'

'No,' I said, humbly. 'I suppose not.'

'So, go on, then, loud mouth . . . teach me!'

It was one of those special times, the Viennese evening. One of those golden times, better-than-ever-expected. One of those times, so rare and so precious, when it all turns out to be just as you had dreamed.

Abbey looked so beautiful, with her lovely blonde hair piled high on her head, and this gorgeous white dress that she had made for herself. Somebody had brought along a camera and kept taking photographs. There's one of me and Pilch doing the polka (just showing off: we really fancied ourselves), one of Zoot hamming it up with Big Jane, one of Little Jane and Andy attempting a waltz; and one of David and Abbey when they didn't know the camera was on them. Everyone said that they made the perfect couple.

Abbey's at university now. She's in her fifth term, and finally starting to settle down. There was a time when she was going to run away. She had this crazy idea of setting out to sea, all by herself, in a dinghy, and just sailing aimlessly until she arrived somewhere. Or until the sharks got her. She was at the stage, then, when she simply couldn't see any point in going on.

She's coming through it. Last time we met, at a school reunion, she was telling me about these new friends that she's made. One of them is a boy. He's called Gary. I couldn't help noticing that his name cropped up far more frequently than anyone else's. I rather think Abbey is on the way to an emotional involvement, and of course I'm glad for her sake even though, just at first, it seemed disloyal—which is nonsense, because it's what David would have wanted.

We talked of David when we met at the reunion; the first time we've been able to bring ourselves to do so. We talked quite naturally, not at all in hushed or reverential tones. We cried a lot, but we laughed as well. We even managed to do both together.

Abbey says that that evening of the dance, that golden, beautiful Viennese evening, is one that will always be with her. She says it's one of those memories that 'time will not wither, nor custom stale'.

She also has a private memory; one that makes her blush and that she doesn't want to talk about. I suspect it's rather too personal for sharing, so although I'm naturally curious I resist the temptation to press her and content myself with imagining. Whatever it is, it's obviously something special, for a funny little smile plays across her lips as she mentions it. She says that that, and the Viennese evening, are what she will remember above all else.

We don't know what Zoot will remember because when Zoot left school he went off to Israel to live on a kibbutz and we haven't heard from him for ages, but knowing Zoot it will probably be something like a cricket match, or the time that he and David got drunk and paddled in the sea (and said that I had big knockers). Something like that.

Me, I shall remember that day on the beach, when David held my hand and I taught him how to dance. I didn't do it terribly well—I'm not really sure that David was any more proficient when we'd finished than when we'd started—but at the end he kissed me and said, 'Robyn, you're a catharsis!'

I didn't know what the word meant until later, when I asked Pop. Pop looked at me over his spectacles and said, 'Purgative'; but when I looked it up in the dictionary I saw that it could also mean 'the releasing of a pent-up emotion'.

I like to think that that was the way David was using it. I shall always remember him kissing me and telling me I was a catharsis.

Always. For as long as I live.